THE FARTHEST SHORE

BY THE SAME AUTHOR:

A WIZARD OF EARTHSEA

THE TOMBS OF ATUAN

THE FARTHEST SHORE

by

Ursula Le Guin

VICTOR GOLLANCZ LTD
LONDON, 1973

Printed in Great Britain
by Ebenezer Baylis and Son Limited
The Trinity Press, Worcester, and London

Contents

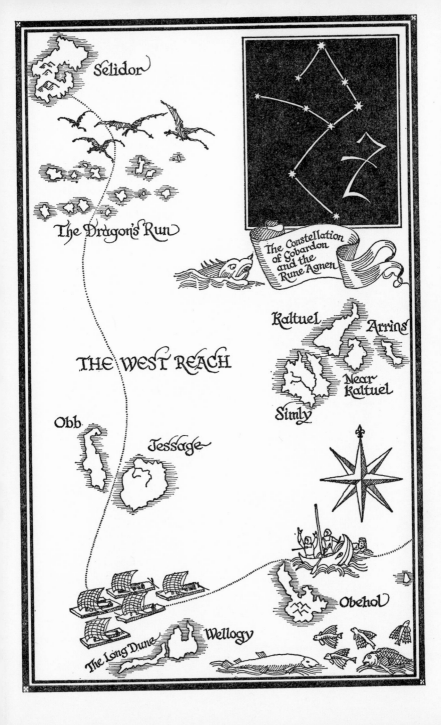

1 *The Rowan Tree*

In the Court of the Fountain the sun of March shone through young leaves of ash and elm, and water leapt and fell through shadow and clear light. About that roofless court stood four high walls of stone. Behind those were rooms and courts, passages, corridors, towers, and at last the heavy outmost walls of the Great House of Roke, which would stand any assault of war, or earthquake, or the sea itself, being built not only of stone, but of incontestable magic. For Roke is the Isle of the Wise, where the art magic is taught; and the Great House is the school and central place of wizardry; and the central place of the House is that small court far within the walls, where the fountain plays and the trees stand in rain or sun or starlight.

The tree nearest the fountain, a well-grown rowan, had humped and cracked the marble pavement with its roots. Veins of bright green moss filled the cracks, spreading up from the grassy plot around the basin. A boy sat there on the low hump of marble and moss, his gaze following the fall of the fountain's central jet. He was nearly a man, but still a boy; slender, dressed richly. His face might have been cast in golden bronze, it was so finely moulded and so still.

Behind him, fifteen feet away perhaps, under the trees at the other end of the small central lawn, a man stood, or seemed to stand. It was hard to be certain in that flickering shift of shadow and warm light. Surely he was there, a man in white, standing motionless. As the boy watched the fountain, so he watched the boy. There was no sound or movement but the play of leaves and the play of the water and its continual song.

The man walked forward. A wind stirred the rowan tree and moved its newly-opened leaves. The boy leapt to his feet, lithe and startled. He faced the man and bowed to him. "My Lord Archmage," he said.

The man stopped before him, a short, straight, vigorous figure in a hooded cloak of white wool. Above the folds of the laid-down hood his face was reddish-dark, hawk-nosed, seamed on one cheek with old scars. The eyes were bright and fierce. Yet he spoke gently. "It's a pleasant place to sit, the Court of the Fountain," he said, and, forestalling the boy's apology, "You have travelled far, and have not rested. Sit down again."

He knelt on the white rim of the basin and held out his hand to the ring of glittering drops that fell from the higher bowl of the fountain, letting the water run through his fingers. The boy sat down again on the humped tiles, and for a minute neither spoke.

"You are the son of the Prince of Enlad and the Enlades," the Archmage said, "heir of the Principality of Morred. There is no older heritage in all Earthsea, and none fairer. I have seen the orchards of Enlad in the Spring, and the golden roofs of Berila. . . . How are you called?"

"I am called Arren."

"That would be a word in the dialect of your land. What is it in our common speech?"

The boy said, "Sword."

The Archmage nodded. There was silence again, and then the boy said, not boldly, but without timidity, "I had thought the Archmage knew all languages."

The man shook his head, watching the fountain.

"And all names. . . ."

"All names? Only Segoy who spoke the First Word, raising up the isles from the deep sea, knew all names. To be sure," and the bright, fierce gaze was on Arren's face, "if I needed to know your true name, I would know it. But there's no need. Arren I will call you; and I am Sparrowhawk. Tell me, how was your voyage here?"

"Too long."

"The winds blew ill?"

"The winds blew fair, but the news I bear is ill, Lord Sparrowhawk."

"Tell it, then," the Archmage said, gravely, but like one yielding to a child's impatience; and while Arren spoke, he looked again at the crystal curtain of water-drops falling from the upper basin into the lower, not as if he did not listen, but as if he listened to more than the boy's words.

"You know, my lord, that the prince my father is a wizardly man, being of the lineage of Morred, and having spent a year here on Roke in his youth. Some power he has, and knowledge, though he seldom uses his arts, being concerned with the ruling and ordering of his realm, and the governance of cities, and matters of trade. The fleets of our island go out westward, even into the West Reach, trading for sapphires and ox-hides and tin, and early this winter a sea-captain returned to our city Berila with a tale that came to my father's ears, so that he had the man sent for and heard him tell it." The boy spoke quickly, with assurance. He had been trained by civil, courtly people, and did not have the self-consciousness of the young. "The sea-captain said that on the isle of Narveduen, which is some five hundred miles west of us by the ship-lanes, there was no more magic. Spells had no power there, he said, and the words of wizardry were forgotten. My father asked him if it was that all the sorcerers and witches had left that isle, and he answered, No: there were some there who had been sorcerers, but they cast no more spells, not even so much as a charm for kettle-mending or the finding of a lost needle. And my father asked, Were not the folk of Narveduen dismayed? And the sea-captain said again, No, they seemed uncaring. And indeed, he said, there was sickness among them, and their autumn harvest had been poor, and still they seemed careless. He said—I was there, when he spoke to the prince—he said, 'They were like sick men, like a man who has been told he must die within the year, and tells himself it is not true, and he will live forever. They go about,' he said, 'without looking at the world.' When other traders returned they repeated the tale that Narveduen had become a poor land and had lost the arts of wizardry. But all this was mere tales of the Reach, which are always strange, and only my father gave it much thought. Then in the New Year, in the Festival of the Lambs that we hold in Enlad, when the shepherds' wives come into the city bringing the firstlings of the flocks, my father named the wizard Root to say the spells of increase over the lambs. But Root came back to our hall distressed, and laid his staff down, and said, 'My lord, I cannot say the spells.' My father questioned him, but he could say only, 'I have forgotten the words and the patterning.' So my father went to the market-place and said the spells himself, and the festival was completed. But I saw him come home to the palace that evening, and he looked grim and weary, and he said to me, 'I said the words, but I do not know if they had meaning.' And indeed there's trouble among the flocks this spring, the ewes dying in birth, and many lambs born dead, and some are . . . deformed." The boy's easy, eager voice dropped; he winced as he said the word, and swallowed. "I saw some of them," he said. There was a pause.

"My father believes that this matter, and the tale of Narveduen, show some evil at work in our part of the world. He desires the counsel of the Wise."

"That he sent you proves that his desire is urgent," said the

Archmage. "You are his only son, and the voyage from Enlad to Roke is not short. Is there more to tell?"

"Only some old wives' tales from the hills."

"What do the old wives say?"

"That all the fortunes witches read in smoke and water-pools tell of ill, and that their love-potions go amiss. But these are people without true wizardry."

"Fortune-telling and love-potions are not of much account, but old women are worth listening to. Well, your message will indeed be discussed by the Masters of Roke. But I do not know, Arren, what counsel they may give your father. For Enlad is not the first land from which such tidings have come."

Arren's trip from the north, down past the great isle Havnor and through the Inmost Sea to Roke, was his first voyage. Only in these last few weeks had he seen lands that were not his own homeland, and become aware of distance and diversity, and recognised that there was a great world beyond the pleasant hills of Enlad, and many people in it. He was not yet used to thinking widely, and so it was a while before he understood.

"Where else?" he asked then, a little dismayed. For he had hoped to bring a prompt cure home to Enlad.

"In the South Reach, first. Latterly even in the south of the Archipelago, in Wathort. There is no more magic done in Wathort, men say. It is hard to be sure. That land has long been rebellious and piratical, and to hear a Southern trader is to hear a liar, as they say. Yet the story is always the same: The springs of wizardry have run dry."

"But here on Roke—"

"Here on Roke we have felt nothing of this. We are defended here from storm, and change, and all ill chance. Too well defended, perhaps. Prince, what will you do now?"

"I shall go back to Enlad when I can bring my father some clear word of the nature of this evil, and of its remedy."

Once more the Archmage looked at him, and this time, for all his training, Arren looked away. He did not know why, for there was nothing unkind in the gaze of those dark eyes. They were impartial, calm, compassionate.

All in Enlad looked up to his father, and he was his father's son. No man had ever looked at him thus, not as Arren Prince of Enlad son of the Ruling Prince, but as Arren alone. He did not like to think that he feared the Archmage's gaze, but he could not meet it. It seemed to enlarge the world yet again around him, and now not only Enlad sank to insignificance, but he himself, so that in the eyes of the Archmage he was only a small figure, very small, in a vast scene of sea-girt lands over which hung darkness.

He sat picking at the vivid moss that grew in the cracks of the marble flagstones, and presently he said, hearing his voice, which had deepened only in the last couple of years, sound thin and husky: "And I shall do as you bid me."

"Your duty is to your father, not to me," the Archmage said.

His eyes were still on Arren, and now the boy looked up. As he had made his act of submission he had forgotten himself, and now he saw the Archmage: the greatest wizard of all Earthsea, the man who had capped the Black Well of Fundaur, and won the Ring of Erreth-Akbe from the Tombs of Atuan, and built the deep-founded seawall of Nepp; the sailor who knew the seas from Astowell to Selidor; the only living Dragonlord. There he knelt beside a fountain, a short man and not young, a quiet-voiced man, with eyes as deep as evening.

Arren scrambled up from sitting and knelt down formally on both knees, all in haste. "My lord," he said stammering, "let me serve you!"

His self-assurance was gone, his face was flushed, his voice shook.

At his hip he wore a sword in a sheath of new leather figured with inlay of red and gold; but the sword itself was plain, with a worn cross-hilt of silvered bronze. This he drew forth, all in haste, and offered the hilt to the Archmage, as a liegeman to his prince.

The Archmage did not put out his hand to touch the sword-hilt. He looked at it, and at Arren. "That is yours, not mine," he said. "And you are no man's servant."

"But my father said that I might stay on Roke until I learned what this evil is, and maybe some mastery—I have no skill, I don't think I have any power, but there were mages among my forefathers—if I might in some way learn to be of use to you—"

"Before your ancestors were mages," the Archmage said, "they were kings."

He stood up and came with silent, vigorous step to Arren, and taking the boy's hand made him rise. "I thank you for your offer of service, and though I do not accept it now, yet I may, when we have taken counsel on these matters. The offer of a generous spirit is not one to refuse lightly. Nor is the sword of the son of Morred to be lightly turned aside! . . . Now go. The lad who brought you here will see that you eat, and bathe, and rest. Go on," and he pushed Arren gently between the shoulder blades, a familiarity no one had ever taken before, and which the young prince would have resented from anyone else; but the Archmage's touch was like an accolade.

Arren was an active boy, delighting in games, taking pride and pleasure in the skills of body and mind, apt at his duties of ceremony and governing, which were neither light nor simple. Yet he had never given himself entirely to anything. All had come easy to him, and he had done all easily; it had all been a game, and he had played at loving. But now the depths of him were wakened, not by a game or dream, but by honour, danger, wisdom, by a scarred face and a quiet voice and a dark hand holding, careless of its power, the staff of yew that bore near the grip, in silver set in the black wood, the Lost Rune of the Kings.

So the first step out of childhood is made all at once, without looking before or behind, without caution, and nothing held in reserve.

Forgetting courtly farewells he hurried to the doorway, awkward, radiant, obedient. And Ged the Archmage watched him go.

Ged stood a while by the fountain under the ash tree, then raised his face to the sunwashed sky. "A gentle messenger for bad news," he said half aloud, as if talking to the fountain. It did not listen, but went on talking in its own silver tongue, and he listened to it a while. Then going to another doorway, which Arren had not seen, and which indeed very few eyes would have seen no matter how close they looked, he said, "Master Doorkeeper."

A little man of no age appeared. Young he was not, so that one had to call him old, but the word did not suit him. His face was dry, and coloured like ivory, and he had a pleasant smile that made long curves in his cheeks. "What's the matter, Ged?" said he.

For they were alone, and he was one of the seven persons in the world who knew the Archmage's name. The others were the Master Namer of Roke; and Ogion the Silent, the wizard of Re Albi, who long ago on the mountain of Gont had given Ged that name; and the White Lady of Gont, Tenar of the Ring; and a village wizard in Iffish called Vetch; and in Iffish again, a house-carpenter's wife, mother of three girls, ignorant of all sorcery but wise in other things, who was called Yarrow; and finally, on the other side of Earthsea, in the farthest west, two dragons: Orm Embar and Kalessin.

"We should meet tonight," the Archmage said. "I'll go to the Patterner. And I'll send to Kurremkarmerruk, so that he'll put his lists away and let his students rest one evening, and come to us, if not in flesh. Will you see to the others?"

"Aye," said the Doorkeeper, smiling, and was gone; and the

Archmage also was gone; and the fountain talked to itself all serene and never ceasing in the sunlight of early spring.

Somewhere to the west of the Great House of Roke, and often somewhat south of it, the Immanent Grove is usually to be seen. There is no place for it on maps, and there is no way to it except for those who know the way to it. But even novices and townsfolk and farmers can see it, always at a certain distance, a wood of high trees whose leaves have a hint of gold in their greenness even in the spring. And they consider—the novices, the townsfolk, the farmers—that the Grove moves about in a mystifying manner. But in this they are mistaken, for the Grove does not move. Its roots are the roots of being. It is all the rest that moves.

Ged walked over the fields from the Great House. He took off his white cloak, for the sun was at noon. A farmer ploughing a brown hillside raised his hand in salute, and Ged replied the same way. Small birds went up into the air and sang. The sparkweed was just coming into flower in the fallows and beside the roads. Far up, a hawk cut a wide arc on the sky. Ged glanced up, and raised his hand again. Down shot the bird in a rush of windy feathers and stooped straight to the offered wrist, gripping with yellow claws. It was no sparrowhawk but a big Enderfalcon of Roke, a white-and-brown-barred fishing hawk. It looked sidelong at the Archmage with one round, bright-gold eye, then clashed its hooked beak and stared at him straight on with both round, bright-gold eyes. "Fearless," the man said to it in the tongue of the Making, "fearless."

The big hawk beat its wings and gripped with its talons, gazing at him.

"Go then, brother, fearless one."

The farmer, away off on the hillside under the bright sky, had stopped to watch. Once last autumn he had watched the Archmage take a wild bird on his wrist, and then in the next moment had seen no man, but two hawks mounting on the wind.

This time they parted as the farmer watched: the bird to the high air, the man walking on across the muddy fields.

He came to the path that led to the Immanent Grove, a path that led always straight and direct no matter how time and the world bent awry about it, and following it came soon into the shadow of the trees.

The trunks of some of these were vast. Seeing them one could believe at last that the Grove never moved: they were like immemorial towers grey with years, their roots were like the roots of mountains. Yet these, the most ancient, were some of them thin of leaf, with branches that had died. They were not immortal. Among the giants grew sapling trees, tall and vigorous with bright crowns of foliage, and seedlings, slight leafy wands no taller than a girl.

The ground beneath the trees was soft, rich with the rotten leaves of all the years. Ferns and small woodland plants grew in it, but there was no kind of tree but the one, which had no name in the Hardic tongue of Earthsea. Under the branches the air smelled earthy and fresh, and had a taste in the mouth like live springwater.

In a glade which had been made years before by the falling of an enormous tree Ged met the Master Patterner, who lived within the Grove and seldom or never came forth from it. His hair was yellow as butter; he was no Archipelagan. Since the restoral of the Ring of Erreth-Akbe, the barbarians of Kargad had ceased their forays and had struck some bargains of trade and peace with the Inner Lands. They were not friendly folk, and held aloof. But now and then a young warrior or merchant's son came westward by himself, drawn by love of adventure or craving to learn wizardry. Such had been the Master Patterner ten years ago, a sword-begirt, red-plumed young savage from Karego-At, arriving at Roke on a rainy morning and telling the

Doorkeeper in imperious and scanty Hardic, "I come to learn!" And now he stood in the green-gold light under the trees, a tall man and fair, with long fair hair, and strange green eyes, the Master Patterner of Earthsea.

It may be that he too knew Ged's name, but if so he never spoke it. They greeted each other in silence.

"What are you watching there?" the Archmage asked, and the other answered, "A spider."

Between two tall grassblades in the clearing a spider had spun a web, a circle delicately suspended. The silver threads caught the sunlight. In the centre the spinner waited, a grey-black thing no larger than the pupil of an eye.

"She too is a patterner," Ged said, studying the artful web.

"What is evil?" asked the younger man.

The round web, with its black centre, seemed to watch them both.

"A web we men weave," Ged answered.

In this wood no birds sang. It was silent in the noon light, and hot. About them stood the trees and shadows.

"There is word from Narveduen and Enlad: the same."

"South and south-west. North and north-west," said the Patterner, never looking from the round web.

"We shall come here this evening. This is the best place for counsel."

"I have no counsel." The Patterner looked now at Ged, and his greenish eyes were cold. "I am afraid," he said. "There is fear. There is fear at the roots."

"Aye," said Ged. "We must look to the deep springs, I think. We have enjoyed the sunlight too long, basking in that peace which the healing of the Ring brought, accomplishing small things, fishing the shallows. Tonight we must question the depths." And so he left the Patterner alone, gazing still at the spider in the sunny grass.

At the edge of the Grove, where the leaves of the great trees reached out over ordinary ground, he sat with his back against a mighty root, his staff across his knees. He shut his eyes as if resting, and sent a sending of his spirit over the hills and fields of Roke, northward, to the sea-assaulted cape where the Isolate Tower stands.

"Kurremkarmerruk," he said in spirit, and the Master Namer looked up from the thick book of names of roots and herbs and leaves and seeds and petals which he was reading to his pupils, and said, "I am here, my lord."

Then he listened, a big, thin, old man, white-haired under his dark hood; and the students at their writing-tables in the tower room looked up at him, and glanced at one another.

"I will come," Kurremkarmerruk said, and bent his head to his book again, saying, "Now the petal of the flower of moly hath a name, which is *iebera*, and so also the sepal, which is *partonath*; and stem and leaf and root hath each his name. . . ."

But under his tree the Archmage Ged, who knew all the names of moly, withdrew his sending, and stretched out his legs more comfortably, and kept his eyes shut, and presently fell asleep in the leaf-spotted sunlight.

2   *The Masters of Roke*

The School on Roke is where boys who show promise in sorcery are sent from all the Inner Lands of Earthsea to learn the highest arts of magic. There they become proficient in the various kinds of sorcery, learning names, and runes, and skills, and spells, and what should and what should not be done, and why. And there, after long practice, and if hand and mind and spirit all keep pace together, they may be named wizard, and receive the staff of power. True wizards are made only on Roke; and since there are sorcerers and witches on all the isles, and the uses of magic are as needful to their people as bread and as delightful as music, so the School of Wizardry is a place held in reverence. The nine mages who are the Masters of the School are considered the equals of the great princes of the Archipelago. Their master, the warden of Roke, the Archmage, is held to be accountable to no man at all, except the King of All the Isles: and that only by an act of fealty, by heart's gift, for not even a king could constrain so great a mage to serve the common law, if his will were otherwise. Yet even in the kingless centuries the Archmages of Roke kept fealty and served that common law. All was done on Roke as it had been done for many hundred years; a place safe from all trouble it seemed, and the laughter of boys rang in the echoing courts and down the broad, cold corridors of the Great House.

Arren's guide about the School was a stocky lad whose cloak was clasped at the neck with silver, in token that he had passed his novicehood and was a proven sorcerer, studying to gain his staff. He was called Gamble. "Because," said he, "my parents had six girls, and the seventh child, my father said, was a gamble against Fate." He was an agreeable companion, quick of mind and tongue. At another time Arren would have enjoyed his humour, but today his mind was too full. He did not pay him very much attention, in fact. And Gamble, with a natural wish to be given credit for existence, began to take advantage of the guest's absentmindedness. He told him strange facts about the School, and then told him strange lies about the School, and to all of them Arren said "Oh yes" or "I see", until Gamble thought him a royal idiot.

"Of course they don't cook in here," he said, showing Arren past the huge stone kitchens all alive with the glitter of copper cauldrons and the clatter of chopping-knives and the eye-prickling smell of onions. "It's just for show. We come to the refectory, and everybody charms up whatever he wants to eat. Saves dishwashing, too."

"Yes, I see," said Arren politely.

"Of course novices who haven't learned the spells yet often lose a good deal of weight, their first months here; but they learn. There's one boy from Havnor who always tries for roast chicken, but all he ever gets is millet mush. He can't seem to get his spells past millet mush. He did get a dried haddock along with it, yesterday." Gamble was getting hoarse with the effort to push his guest into incredulity. He gave up, and stopped talking.

"Where . . . what land does the Archmage come from?" said that guest, not even looking at the mighty gallery through which they were walking, all carven on wall and arched ceiling with the Thousand-Leaved Tree.

"Gont," said Gamble. "He was a village goatherd there."

Now, at this plain and well-known fact, the boy from Enlad turned and looked with disapproving unbelief at Gamble. "A goatherd?"

"That's what most Gontishmen are, unless they're pirates or sorcerers. I didn't say he was a goatherd now, you know!"

"But how would a goatherd become Archmage?"

"The same way a prince would! By coming to Roke and outdoing all the Masters, by stealing the Ring in Atuan, by sailing the Dragons' Run, by being the greatest wizard since Erreth-Akbe—how else?"

They came out of the gallery by the north door. Late afternoon lay warm and bright on the furrowed hills and the roofs of Thwil Town and the bay beyond. There they stood to talk. Gamble said, "Of course that's all long ago, now. He hasn't done much since he was named Archmage. They never do. They just sit on Roke and watch the Equilibrium, I suppose. And he's quite old now."

"Old? How old?"

"Oh, forty or fifty."

"Have you seen him?"

"Of course I've seen him," Gamble said sharply. The royal idiot seemed also to be a royal snob.

"Often?"

"No. He keeps to himself. But when I first came to Roke I saw him, in the Fountain Court."

"I spoke with him there today," Arren said. His tone made Gamble look at him, and then answer him fully: "It was three years ago. And I was so frightened I never really looked at him. I was pretty young, of course. But it's hard to see things clearly in there. I remember his voice, mostly, and the fountain running." After a moment he added, "He does have a Gontish accent."

"If I could speak to dragons in their own language," Arren said, "I wouldn't care about my accent."

At that Gamble looked at him with a degree of approval, and asked, "Did you come here to join the school, prince?"

"No. I carried a message from my father to the Archmage."

"Enlad is one of the Principalities of the Kingship, isn't it?"

"Enlad, Ilien, and Way. Havnor and Éa, once, but the line of descent from the kings has died out in those lands. Ilien traces the descent from Gemal Sea-born through Maharion. Way, from Akambar and the House of Shelieth. Enlad, the oldest, from Morred through his son Serriadh and the House of Enlad."

Arren recited these genealogies with a dreamy air, like a well-trained scholar whose mind is on another subject.

"Do you think we'll see a king in Havnor again in our lifetime?"

"I never thought about it much."

"In Ark, where I come from, people think about it. We're part of the Principality of Ilien now, you know, since peace was made. How long has it been, seventeen years, or eighteen, since the Ring of the King's Rune was returned to the Tower of the Kings in Havnor? Things were better for a while then, but now they're worse than ever. It's time there was a king again on the throne of Earthsea, to wield the Sign of Peace. People are tired of wars and raids and merchants who overprice and princes who overtax and all the confusion of unruly powers. Roke guides, but it can't rule. The Balance lies here, but the Power should lie in the king's hands."

Gamble spoke with real interest, all foolery set aside, and Arren's attention was finally caught. "Enlad is a rich and peaceful land," he said slowly. "It has never entered into these rivalries. We hear of the troubles in other lands. But there's been no king on the throne in Havnor since Maharion died: eight hundred years. Would the lands indeed accept a king?"

"If he came in peace and in strength; if Roke and Havnor recognised his claim."

"And there is a prophecy that must be fulfilled, isn't there? Maharion said that the next king must be a mage."

"The Master Chanter's a Havnorian and interested in the matter, and he's been dinning the words into us for three years now. Maharion said, *He shall inherit my throne who has crossed the dark land living and come to the far shores of the day.*"

"Therefore a mage."

"Yes, since only a wizard or mage can go among the dead in the dark land and return. Though they do not *cross* it. At least, they always speak of it as if it had only one boundary, and beyond that, no end. What are *the far shores of the day*, then? But so runs the prophecy of the Last King, and therefore some day one will be born to fulfil it. And Roke will recognise him, and the fleets and armies and nations will come together to him. Then there will be majesty again in the centre of the world, in the Tower of the Kings in Havnor. I would come to such a one, I would serve a true king with all my heart and all my art," said Gamble, and then laughed and shrugged, lest Arren think he spoke with over-much emotion. But Arren looked at him with friendliness, thinking, "He would feel towards the king as I do towards the Archmage." Aloud he said, "A king would need such men as you about him."

They stood, each thinking his own thoughts, yet companionable, until a gong rang sonorous in the Great House behind them.

"There!" said Gamble. "Lentil and onion soup tonight. Come on."

"I thought you said they didn't cook," said Arren, still dreamy, following.

"Oh, sometimes—by mistake—"

No magic was involved in the dinner, though plenty of substance was. After it they walked out over the fields in the soft blue of the dusk. "This is Roke Knoll," Gamble said as they began to climb a rounded hill. The dewy grass brushed their legs, and down by the marshy Thwilburn there was a chorus of little toads to welcome the first warmth and the shortening, starry nights.

There was a mystery in that ground. Gamble said softly, "This hill was the first that stood above the sea, when the First Word was spoken."

"And it will be the last to sink, when all things are unmade," said Arren.

"Therefore a safe place to stand on," Gamble said, shaking off awe; but then he cried, awestruck, "Look! The Grove!"

South of the Knoll a great light was revealed on the earth, like moonrise, but the thin moon was already setting westward over the hill's top; and there was a flickering in this radiance, like the movement of leaves in the wind.

"What is it?"

"It comes from the Grove—the Masters must be there. They say it burned so, with a light like moonlight, all night, when they met to choose the Archmage five years ago. But why are they meeting now? Is it the news you brought?"

"It may be," said Arren.

Gamble, excited and uneasy, wanted to return to the Great House to hear any rumour of what the Council of the Masters portended. Arren went with him, but looked back often at that strange radiance till the slope hid it, and there was only the new moon setting, and the stars of spring.

Alone in the dark in the stone cell that was his sleeping-room, Arren lay with eyes open. He had slept on a bed all his life, under soft furs; even in the twenty-oared galley in which he had come from Enlad they had provided their young prince with more comfort than this—a straw pallet on the stone floor, and a ragged blanket of felt. But he noticed none of it. "I am at the centre of the world," he thought. "The Masters are talking in the holy place. What will they do? Will they weave a great magic to save magic? Can it be true that wizardry is dying out of the world? Is there a danger that threatens even Roke? I will stay here. I will not go home. I would rather sweep his room than be a prince in Enlad. Would he let me stay as a novice? But perhaps there will be no more teaching of the art magic, no more learning of the true names of things. My father has the gift of wizardry, but I do not; perhaps it is indeed dying out of the world. Yet I would stay near *him*, even if he lost his power and his art. Even if I never saw him. Even if he never said another word to me." But his ardent imagination swept him on past that, so that in a moment he saw himself face to face with the Archmage once more in the court beneath the rowan tree, and the sky was dark, and the tree leafless, and the fountain silent; and he said, "My lord, the storm is on us, yet I will stay by thee, and serve thee," and the Archmage smiled at him. . . . But there imagination failed, for he had not seen that dark face smile.

In the morning he rose, feeling that yesterday he had been a boy, today he was a man. He was ready for anything. But when it came, he stood gaping. "The Archmage wishes to speak to you, Prince Arren," said a little novice-lad at his doorway, waited a moment, and ran off before Arren could collect his wits to answer.

He made his way down the tower staircase and through stone corridors towards the Fountain Court, not knowing where he should go. An old man met him in the corridor, smiling so that deep furrows ran down his cheeks from nose to chin: the same who had met him yesterday at the door of the Great House when he first came up from the harbour, and had required him to say his true name before he entered. "Come this way," said the Master Doorkeeper.

The halls and passages in this part of the building were silent, empty of the rush and racket of the boys that enlivened the rest. Here one felt the great age of the walls. The enchantment with which the ancient stones were laid and protected was here palpable. Runes were graven on the walls at intervals, cut deep, some inlaid with silver. Arren had learned the Runes of Hardic from his father, but none of these did he know, though certain of them seemed to hold a meaning that he almost knew, or had known and could not quite remember.

"Here you are, lad," said the Doorkeeper, who made no account of titles such as Lord or Prince. Arren followed him into a long, low-beamed room, where on one side a fire burned in a stone hearth, its flames reflecting in the oaken floor, and on the other side pointed windows let in the heavy light of a foggy morning. Before the hearth stood a group of men. All looked at him as he entered, but among them he saw only one, the Archmage. He stopped, and bowed, and stood dumb.

"These are the Masters of Roke, Arren," said the Archmage, "seven of the nine. The Patterner will not leave his Grove, and the Namer is in his tower, thirty miles to the north. All of them know your errand here. My lords, this is the son of Morred."

No pride roused in Arren at that phrase, but only a kind of dread. He was proud of his lineage, but thought of himself only as an heir of princes, one of the House of Enlad. Morred, from whom that house descended, had been dead two thousand years. His deeds were matter of legends, not of this present world. It was as if the Archmage had named him son of myth, inheritor of dreams.

He did not dare look up at the faces of the eight mages. He stared at the iron-shod foot of the Archmage's staff, and felt the blood ringing in his ears.

"Come, let us breakfast together," said the Archmage, and led them to a table set beneath the windows. There was milk and sour beer, bread, new butter, and cheese. Arren sat with them and ate.

He had been among noblemen, landholders, rich merchants, all his life. His father's hall in Berila was full of them: men who owned much, who bought and sold much, rich in the things of the world. They ate meat and drank wine, and talked loud;

many disputed, many flattered, most sought something for themselves. Young as he was, Arren had learned a good deal about the manners and disguises of humanity. But he had never been among such men as these. They ate bread, and talked little, and their faces were quiet. If they sought something, it was not for themselves. Yet they were men of great power: that, too, Arren recognised.

Sparrowhawk the Archmage sat at the head of the table and seemed to listen to what was said, and yet there was a silence about him, and no one spoke to him. Arren was let alone also, so that he had time to recover himself. On his left was the Doorkeeper, and on his right a grey-haired man with a kindly look, who said to him at last, "We are countrymen, Prince Arren. I was born in eastern Enlad, by the Forest of Aol."

"I have hunted in that forest," Arren replied, and they spoke together a little of the woods and towns of the Isle of the Myths, so that Arren was comforted by the memory of his home.

When the meal was done they drew together once more before the hearth, some sitting and some standing, and there was a little silence.

"Last night," the Archmage said, "we met in council. Long we talked, yet resolved nothing. I would hear you say now, in the morning light, whether you uphold or gainsay your judgment of the night."

"That we resolved nothing," said the Master Herbal, a stocky, dark-skinned man with calm eyes, "is itself a judgment. In the Grove are patterns found; but we found nothing there but argument."

"Only because we could not see the pattern plain," said the grey-haired mage of Enlad, the Master Changer. "We do not know enough. Rumours from Wathort; news from Enlad. Strange news, and should be looked to. But to raise a great fear on so little a foundation is unneedful. Our power is not threatened only because a few sorcerers have forgotten their spells."

"So say I," said a lean, keen-eyed man, the Master Windkey. "Have we not all our powers? Do not the trees of the Grove grow and put forth leaves? Do not the storms of heaven obey our word? Who can fear for the art of wizardry, which is the oldest of the arts of man?"

"No man," said the Master Summoner, deep-voiced and tall, young, with a dark and noble face, "no man, no power, can bind the action of wizardry, or still the words of power. For they are the very words of the Making, and one who could silence them could unmake the world."

"Aye, and one who could do that would not be on Wathort or Narveduen," said the Changer. "He would be here at the gates of Roke, and the end of the world would be at hand! We've not to come to that pass yet."

"Yet there is something wrong," said another, and they looked at him: deep-chested, solid as an oaken cask, he sat by the fire, and the voice came from him soft and true as the note of a great bell. He was the Master Chanter. "Where is the king that should be in Havnor? Roke is not the heart of the world. That tower is, on which the sword of Erreth-Akbe is set, and in which stands the throne of Serriadh, of Akambar, of Maharion. Eight hundred years has the heart of the world been empty! We have the crown, but no king to wear it. We have the Lost Rune, the King's Rune, the Rune of Peace, restored to us, but have we peace? Let there be a king upon the throne, and we will have peace, and even in the farthest Reaches the sorcerers will practise their arts with untroubled mind, and there will be order, and a due season to all things."

"Aye," said the Master Hand, a slight, quick man, modest of bearing but with clear and seeing eyes. "I am with you, Chanter. What wonder that wizardry goes astray, when all else goes astray? If the whole flock wander, will our black sheep stay by the fold?"

At that the Doorkeeper laughed, but he said nothing.

"Then to you all," said the Archmage, "it seems that there is nothing very wrong; or if there is, it lies in this, that our lands are ungoverned or ill-governed, so that all the arts and high skills of men suffer from neglect. With that much I agree. Indeed it is because the South is all but lost to peaceful commerce, that we must depend on rumour; and who has any safe word from the West Reach, save this from Narveduen? If ships went forth and came back safely as of old, if our lands of Earthsea were well-knit, we might know how things stand in the remote places, and so could act. And I think we would act! For, my lords, when the Prince of Enlad tells us that he spoke the words of the Making in a spell, and yet did not know their meaning as he spoke them; when the Master Patterner says that there is fear at the roots, and will say no more: is this so little a foundation for anxiety? When a storm begins, it is only a little cloud on the horizon."

"You have a sense for the black things, Sparrowhawk," said the Doorkeeper. "You ever did. Say what you think is wrong."

"I do not know. There is a weakening of power. There is a want of resolution. There is a dimming of the sun. I feel, my lords—I feel as if we who sit here talking, were all wounded mortally, and while we talk and talk our blood runs softly from our veins. . . ."

"And you would be up and doing."

"I would," said the Archmage.

"Well," said the Doorkeeper, "can the owls keep the hawk from flying?"

"But where would you go?" the Changer asked, and the Chanter answered him: "To seek our king and bring him to his throne!"

The Archmage looked keenly at the Chanter, but answered only, "I would go where the trouble is."

"South, or west," said the Master Windkey.

"And north and east if need be," said the Doorkeeper.

"But you are needed here, my lord," said the Changer. "Rather than to go seeking blindly among unfriendly peoples, on strange seas, would it not be wiser to stay here, where all magic is strong, and find out by your arts what this evil or disorder is?"

"My arts do not avail me," the Archmage said. There was that in his voice which made them all look at him, sober and with uneasy eyes. "I am the Warder of Roke. I do not leave Roke lightly. I wish that your counsel and my own were the same; but that is not to be hoped for, now. The judgment must be mine: and I must go."

"To that judgment we yield," said the Summoner.

"And I go alone. You are the Council of Roke, and it must not be broken. Yet one I will take with me, if he will come." He looked at Arren. "You offered me your service, yesterday. Last night the Master Patterner said, 'Not by chance does any man come to the shores of Roke. Not by chance is a son of Morred the bearer of this news.' And no other word had he for us all the night. Therefore I ask you, Arren, will you come with me?"

"Yes, my lord," said Arren, with a dry throat.

"The prince your father surely would not let you go into this peril," said the Changer somewhat sharply, and to the Archmage, "The lad is young, and not trained in wizardry."

"I have years and spells enough for both of us," Sparrowhawk said in a dry voice. "Arren, what of your father?"

"He would let me go."

"How can you know?" asked the Summoner.

Arren did not know where he was being required to go, nor when, nor why. He was bewildered, and abashed by these grave, honest, terrible men. If he had had time to think he could not

have said anything at all. But he had no time to think
Archmage had asked him, "Will you come with me?"

"When my father sent me here he said to me, 'I fea
time is coming on the world, a time of danger. So I se
rather than any other messenger, for you can judge whet
should ask the help of the Isle of the Wise in this mat
offer the help of Enlad to them.' So if I am needed, the
I am here."

At that he saw the Archmage smile. There was great sv
ness in his smile, though it was brief. "Do you see?" he sai
the seven mages. "Could age, or wizardry, add anything to thi

Arren felt that they looked on him approvingly then, but w
a kind of pondering or wondering look, still. The Summor
spoke, his arched brows straightened to a frown: "I do n
understand it, my lord. That you are bent on going, yes. Yo
have been caged here five years. But always before you wer
alone; you have always gone alone. Why, now, companioned?"

"I never needed help before," said Sparrowhawk, with an
edge of threat or irony in his voice. "And I have found a fit
companion." There was a dangerousness about him, and the tall
Summoner asked him no more questions, though he still
frowned.

But the Master Herbal, calm-eyed and dark like a wise and
patient ox, rose from his seat and stood monumental. "Go, my
lord," he said, "and take the lad. And all our trust goes with
you."

One by one the others gave assent quietly, and by ones and
twos withdrew, until only the Summoner was left of the seven.
"Sparrowhawk," he said, "I do not seek to question your judgment. Only I say: if you are right, if there is imbalance and the
peril of great evil, then a voyage to Wathort, or into the West
Reach, or to world's end, will not be far enough. Where you
may have to go, can you take this companion, and is it fair to
him?"

They stood apart from Arren, and the Summoner's voice was lowered, but the Archmage spoke openly: "It is fair."

"You are not telling me all you know," the Summoner said.

"If I knew, I would speak. I know nothing. I guess much."

"Let me come with you."

"One must guard the gates."

"The Doorkeeper does that—"

"Not only the gates of Roke. Stay here. Stay here, and watch the sunrise to see if it be bright, and watch at the wall of stones to see who crosses it and where their faces are turned. There is a breach, Thorion, there is a break, a wound, and it is this I go to seek. If I am lost then maybe you will find it. But wait. I bid you wait for me." He was speaking now in the Old Speech, the language of the Making, in which all true spells are cast and on which all the great acts of magic depend; but very seldom is it spoken in conversation, except among the dragons. The Summoner made no further argument or protest, but bowed his tall head quietly both to the Archmage and to Arren, and departed.

The fire crackled in the hearth. There was no other sound. Outside the windows the fog pressed formless and dim.

The Archmage stared into the flames, seeming to have forgotten Arren's presence. The boy stood at some distance from the hearth, not knowing if he should take his leave or wait to be dismissed, irresolute and somewhat desolate, feeling again like a small figure in a dark, illimitable, confusing space.

"We'll go first to Hort Town," said Sparrowhawk, turning his back to the fire. "News gathers there from all the South Reach, and we may find a lead. Your ship still waits in the bay. Speak to the master, let him carry word to your father. I think we should leave as soon as may be. At daybreak tomorrow. Come to the steps by the boathouse."

"My lord, what—" His voice stuck a moment. "What is it you seek?"

"I don't know, Arren."

"Then—"

"Then how shall I seek it? Neither do I know that. Maybe it will seek me." He grinned a little at Arren, but his face was like iron in the grey light of the windows.

"My lord," Arren said, and his voice was steady now, "it is true I come of the lineage of Morred, if any tracing of lineage so old be true. And if I can serve you I will account it the greatest chance and honour of my life, and there is nothing I would rather do. But I fear that you mistake me for something more than I am."

"Maybe," said the Archmage.

"I have no great gifts or skills. I can fence with the short sword and the noble sword. I can sail a boat. I know the court-dances and the country-dances. I can mend a quarrel between courtiers. I can wrestle, I am a poor archer, and skilful at the game of net-ball. I can sing, and play the harp and lute. And that is all. There is no more. What use will I be to you? The Master Summoner is right—"

"Ah, you saw that, did you? He's jealous. He claims the privilege of older loyalty."

"And greater skill, my lord."

"Then you'd rather he went with me, and you stayed behind?"

"No! But I fear—"

"Fear what?"

Tears sprang to the boy's eyes. "To fail you," he said.

The Archmage turned around again to the fire. "Sit down, Arren," he said, and the boy came to the stone corner-seat of the hearth. "I did not mistake you for a wizard, or a warrior, or any finished thing. What you are I do not know, though I'm glad to know that you can sail a boat. . . . What you will be, no one knows. But this much I do know: you are the son of Morred and of Serriadh."

Arren was silent. "That is true, my lord," he said at last.

"But . . ." The Archmage said nothing, and he had to finish his sentence: "But I am not Morred. I am only myself."

"You take no pride in your lineage?"

"Yes, I take pride in it—because it makes me a prince, it is a responsibility, a thing that must be lived up to—"

The Archmage nodded once, sharply. "That is what I meant. To deny the past is to deny the future. A man does not make his destiny: he accepts it, or denies it. If the rowan's roots are shallow it bears no crown." At this Arren looked up startled, for his true name, Lebannen, meant the rowan tree. But the Archmage had not said his name. "Your roots are deep," he went on. "You have strength, and you must have room, room to grow. Thus I offer you, instead of a safe trip home to Enlad, an unsafe voyage to an unknown end. You need not come. The choice is yours. But I offer you the choice. For I am tired of safe places, and roofs, and walls around me." He ended abruptly, looking about him with piercing, unseeing eyes. Arren saw the deep restlessness of the man, and it frightened him. Yet fear sharpens exhilaration, and it was with a leap of the heart that he answered, "My lord, I choose to go with you."

Arren left the Great House with his heart and mind full of wonder. He told himself that he was happy, but the word did not seem to suit. He told himself that the Archmage had called him strong, a man of destiny, and that he was proud of such praise; but he was not proud. Why not? The most powerful wizard in the world told him, "Tomorrow we sail to the edge of doom," and he nodded his head and came: should he not feel pride? But he did not. He felt only wonder.

He went down through the steep wandering streets of Thwil Town, found his ship's master on the quays, and said to him, "I sail tomorrow with the Archmage, to Wathort and the South Reach. Tell the Prince my father that when I am released from this service I will come home to Berila."

The ship's Captain looked dour. He knew how the bringer of

36

such news might be received by the Prince of Enlad. "I must have writing about it from your hand, prince," he said. Seeing the justice in that, Arren hurried off—he felt that all must be done instantly—and found a strange little shop where he purchased inkstone and brush and a piece of soft paper, thick as felt; then he hurried back to the quays and sat down on the wharfside to write his parents. When he thought of his mother holding this same piece of paper, reading the letter, a distress came into him. She was a blithe patient woman, but Arren knew that he was the foundation of her contentment, that she longed for his quick return. There was no way to comfort her for his long absence. His letter was dry and brief. He signed with the sword-rune, sealed the letter with a bit of pitch from a caulking-pot nearby, and gave it to the ship's master. Then, "Wait!" he said, as if the ship were ready to set sail that instant, and ran back up the cobbled streets to the strange little shop. He had trouble finding it, for there was something shifty about the streets of Thwil; it almost seemed that the turnings were different every time. He came on the right street at last, and darted into the shop under the strings of red clay beads that ornamented its doorway. When he was buying ink and paper he had noticed, on a tray of clasps and brooches, a silver brooch in the shape of a wild rose; and his mother was called Rose. "I'll buy that," he said in his hasty, princely way.

"Ancient silverwork of the Isle of O. I can see you are a judge of the old crafts," said the shopkeeper, looking at the hilt—not the handsome sheath—of Arren's sword. "That will be four in ivory."

Arren paid the rather high price unquestioning; he had in his purse plenty of the ivory counters that serve as money in the Inner Lands. The idea of a gift for his mother pleased him; the act of buying pleased him; as he left the shop he set his hand on the pommel of his sword, with a touch of swagger.

His father had given him that sword on the eve of his

departure from Enlad. He had received it solemnly, and had worn it, as if it were a duty to wear it, even aboard ship. He was proud of the weight of it at his hip, the weight of its great age on his spirit. For it was the sword of Serriadh who was the son of Morred and Elfarran; there was none older in the world except the sword of Erreth-Akbe, which was set atop the Tower of the Kings in Havnor. This had never been laid away or hoarded up, but worn; yet was unworn by the centuries, unweakened, because it had been forged with a great power of enchantment. Its history said that it never had been drawn, nor ever could be drawn, except in the service of life. For no purpose of bloodlust or revenge or greed, in no war for gain, would it let itself be wielded. From it, the great treasure of his family, Arren had received his use-name: Arrendek he had been called as a child, 'the little Sword'.

He had not used the sword, nor had his father, nor his grandfather. There had been peace in Enlad for a long time.

And now, in the street of the strange town of the Wizards' Isle, the sword's handle felt strange to him when he touched it. It was awkward to his hand, and cold. Heavy, the sword hindered his walk, dragged at him. And the wonder he had felt was still in him but had gone cold. He went back down to the quay, and gave the brooch to the ship's master for his mother, and bade him farewell and a safe voyage home. Turning away he pulled his cloak over the sheath that held the old, unyielding weapon, the deadly thing he had inherited. He did not feel like swaggering any more. "What am I doing?" he said to himself as he climbed the narrow ways, not hurrying now, to the fortress-bulk of the Great House above the town. "How is it that I'm not going home? Why am I seeking something I don't understand, with a man I don't know?"

And he had no answer to his questions.

3   Hort Town

In the darkness before dawn Arren dressed in clothing that had
been given him, seaman's garb, well worn but clean, and hurried
down through the silent halls of the Great House to the eastern
door, carven of horn and dragon's tooth. There the Doorkeeper
let him out, and pointed the way that he should take, smiling
a little. He followed the topmost street of the town and then
a path that led down to the boathouses of the School, south
along the bayshore from the docks of Thwil. He could just
make out his way. Trees, roofs, hills bulked as dim masses
within dimness; the dark air was utterly still and very cold;
everything held still, held itself withdrawn and obscure.
Only over the dark sea eastward was there one faint clear
line: the horizon, tipping momently towards the unseen
sun.

He came to the boathouse steps. No one was there, nothing
moved. In his bulky sailor's coat and wool cap he was warm
enough, but he shivered, standing on the stone steps in the
darkness, waiting.

The boathouses loomed black above black water, and suddenly from them came a dull, hollow sound, a booming knock,
repeated three times. Arren's hair stirred on his scalp. A long
shadow glided out onto the water, silently. It was a boat and it

slid softly towards the pier. Arren ran down the steps and onto the pier, and leapt down into the boat.

"Take the tiller," said the Archmage, a lithe shadowy figure in the prow, "and hold her steady while I get the sail up."

They were out on the water already, the sail opening like a white wing from the mast, catching the growing light. "A west wind to save us rowing out of the bay, that's a parting gift from the Master Windkey, I don't doubt. Watch her, lad, she steers very light! So then. A west wind, and a clear dawn for the Balance-Day of spring."

"Is this boat *Lookfar*?" Arren had heard of the Archmage's boat in songs and tales.

"Aye," said the other, busy with ropes. The boat bucked and veered as the wind freshened; Arren set his teeth and tried to keep her steady.

"She steers very light, but somewhat wilful, lord."

The Archmage laughed. "Let her have her will; she is wise also. Listen, Arren," and he paused, kneeling on the thwart to face Arren, "I am no lord now, nor you a prince. I am a trader called Hawk, and you're my nephew, learning the seas with me, called Arren; for we hail from Enlad. From what town? A large one, lest we meet a townsman."

"Temere, on the south coast? They trade to all the Reaches."

The Archmage nodded.

"But," said Arren cautiously, "you don't have quite the accent of Enlad."

"I know. I have a Gontish accent," his companion said, and laughed, looking up at the brightening east. "But I think I can borrow what I need from you. So we come from Temere in our boat *Dolphin*, and I am neither lord, nor mage, nor Sparrow-hawk, but—how am I called?"

"Hawk, my lord."

Then Arren bit his tongue.

"Practice, nephew," said the Archmage. "It takes practice.

You've never been anything but a prince. While I have been many things, and last of all, and maybe least, an Archmage. . . . We go south looking for emmel-stone, that blue stuff they carve charms of. I know they value it in Enlad. They make it into charms against rheums, sprains, stiff necks, and slips of the tongue."

After a moment Arren laughed, and as he lifted his head the boat lifted on a long wave, and he saw the rim of the sun against the edge of the ocean, a flare of sudden gold, before them.

Sparrowhawk stood with one hand on the mast, for the little boat leaped on the choppy waves, and facing the sunrise of the equinox of spring he chanted. Arren did not know the Old Speech, the tongue of wizards and dragons, but he heard praise and rejoicing in the words, and there was a great striding rhythm in them like the rise and fall of tides or the balance of the day and night each succeeding each forever. Gulls cried on the wind, and the shores of Thwil Bay slid past to right and left, and they entered on the long waves, full of light, of the Inmost Sea.

From Roke to Hort Town is no great voyage, but they spent three nights at sea. The Archmage had been urgent to be gone, but once gone, he was more than patient. The winds turned contrary as soon as they were away from the charmed weather of Roke, but he did not call a mage-wind into their sail, as any weatherworker could have done; instead, he spent hours teaching Arren how to manage the boat in a stiff head-wind, in the rock-fanged sea east of Issel. The second night out it rained, the rough cold rain of March, but he said no spell to keep it off them. On the next night as they lay outside the entrance to Hort Harbour in a calm, cold, foggy darkness, Arren thought about this, and reflected that in this short time he had known him, the Archmage had done no magic at all.

He was a peerless sailor, though. Arren had learned more in three days' sailing with him, than in ten years of boating and racing on Berila Bay. And mage and sailor are not so far apart;

both work with the powers of sky and sea, and bend great winds to the uses of their hands, bringing near what was remote. Archmage or Hawk the sea-trader, it came to much the same thing.

He was a rather silent man, though perfectly goodhumoured. No clumsiness of Arren's fretted him; he was companionable; there could be no better shipmate, Arren thought. But he would go into his own thoughts and be silent for hours on end, and then when he must speak there was a harshness in his voice, and he would look right through Arren. This did not weaken the love the boy felt for him, but maybe it lessened liking somewhat; it was a little awesome. Perhaps Sparrowhawk felt this, for in that foggy night off the shores of Wathort he began to talk to Arren, rather haltingly, about himself. "I do not want to go among men again, tomorrow," he said. "I've been pretending that I am free.... That nothing's wrong in the world. That I'm not Archmage, not even sorcerer. That I'm Hawk of Temere, without responsibilities or privileges, owing nothing to anyone...." He stopped and after a while went on, "Try to choose carefully, Arren, when the great choices must be made. When I was young I had to choose between the life of being and the life of doing. And I leapt at the latter like a trout to a fly. But each deed you do, each act, binds you to itself and to its consequences, and makes you act again, and yet again. Then very seldom do you come upon a space, a time like this, between act and act, when you may stop and simply be. Or wonder who, after all, you are."

How could such a man, thought Arren, be in doubt as to who and what he was? He had believed such doubts were reserved for the young, who had not done anything yet.

They rocked in the great, cool darkness.

"That's why I like the sea," said Sparrowhawk's voice in that darkness.

Arren understood him; but his own thoughts ran ahead, as

they had been doing all these three days and nights, to their quest, the aim of their sailing. And since his companion was in a mood to talk, at last, he asked, "Do you think we will find what we seek in Hort Town?"

Sparrowhawk shook his head, perhaps meaning no, perhaps meaning that he did not know.

"Can it be a kind of pestilence, a plague, that drifts from land to land, blighting the crops and the flocks and men's spirits?"

"A pestilence is a motion of the great balance, of the Equilibrium itself; this is different. There is the stink of evil in it. We may suffer for it when the balance of things rights itself, but we do not lose hope, and forego art, and forget the words of the Making. Nature is not unnatural. This is not a righting of the balance, but an upsetting of it. There is only one creature who can do that."

"A man?" Arren said, tentative.

"We men."

"How?"

"By an unmeasured desire for life."

"For life? But it isn't wrong to want to live?"

"No. But when we crave power over life—endless wealth, unassailable safety, immortality—then desire becomes greed. And if knowledge allies itself to that greed, then comes evil. Then the balance of the world is swayed, and ruin weighs heavy in the scale."

Arren brooded over this a while, and said at last, "Then you think it is a man we seek?"

"A man, and a mage. Aye, I think so."

"But I had thought, from what my father and teachers taught, that the great arts of wizardry were dependent on the Balance, the Equilibrium of things, and so could not be used for evil."

"That," said Sparrowhawk somewhat wryly, "is a debatable

43

point. *Infinite are the arguments of mages.* . . . Every land of Earthsea knows of witches who cast unclean spells, sorcerers who use their art to win riches. But there is more. The Firelord, who sought to undo the darkness and stop the sun at noon, was a great mage; even Erreth-Akbe could scarcely defeat him. The Enemy of Morred was another such. Where he came, whole cities knelt to him; armies fought for him. The spell he wove against Morred was so mighty that even when he was slain it could not be halted, and the island of Soléa was overwhelmed by the sea, and all on it perished. Those were men in whom great strength and knowledge served the will to evil, and fed upon it. Whether the wizardry that serves a better end may always prove the stronger, we do not know. We hope."

There is a certain bleakness in finding hope where one expected certainty. Arren found himself unwilling to stay on these cold summits. He said after a little while, "I see why you say that only men do evil, I think. Even sharks are innocent, they kill because they must."

"That is why nothing else can resist us. Only one thing in the world can resist an evil-hearted man. And that is another man. In our shame is our glory. Only our spirit, which is capable of evil, is capable of overcoming it."

"But the dragons," said Arren. "Do they not do great evil? Are they innocent?"

"The dragons! The dragons are avaricious, insatiable, treacherous; without pity, without remorse. But are they evil? Who am I, to judge the acts of dragons? . . . They are wiser than men are. It is with them as with dreams, Arren. We men dream dreams, we work magic, we do good, we do evil. The dragons do not dream. They are dreams. They do not work magic: it is their substance, their being. They do not do: they are."

"In Serilune," said Arren, "is the skin of Bar Oth, killed by Keor Prince of Enlad three hundred years ago. No dragons have ever come to Enlad since that day. I saw the skin of Bar

Oth. It is heavy as iron, and so large that if it were spread out it would cover all the marketplace of Serilune, they said. The teeth are as long as my forearm. Yet they said Bar Oth was a young dragon, not full grown."

"There is a desire in you," said Sparrowhawk, "to see dragons."

"Yes."

"Their blood is cold, and venomous. You must not look into their eyes. They are older than mankind. . . ." He was silent a while, and then went on, "And though I came to forget or regret all I have ever done, yet I would remember that once I saw the dragons aloft on the wind at sunset above the western isles; and I would be content."

Both were silent then, and there was no sound but the whispering of the water with the boat, and no light. So at last, there on the deep waters, they slept.

In the bright haze of morning they came into Hort Harbour, where a hundred craft were moored or setting forth: fishermen's boats, crabbers, trawlers, trading-ships, two galleys of twenty oars, one great sixty-oared galley in bad repair, and some lean, long sailing-ships with high triangular sails designed to catch the upper airs in the hot calms of the South Reach. "Is that a ship of war?" Arren asked as they passed one of the twenty-oared galleys, and his companion answered, "A slaver, I judge from the chain-bolts in her hold. They sell men, in the South Reach."

Arren pondered this a minute, then went to the gear-box and took from it his sword, which he had wrapped well and stowed away on the morning of their departure. He uncovered it; he stood indecisive, the sheathed sword on his two hands, the belt dangling from it.

"It's no sea-trader's sword," he said. "The scabbard is too fine."

Sparrowhawk, busy at the tiller, shot him a look. "Wear it if you like."

"I thought it might be wise."

"As swords go, that one is wise," said his companion, his eyes alert on their passage through the crowded bay. "Is it not a sword reluctant to be used?"

Arren nodded. "So they say. Yet it has killed. It has killed men." He looked down at the slender, handworn hilt. "It has, but I have not. It makes me feel a fool. It is too much older than I. . . . I shall take my knife," he ended, and rewrapping the sword shoved it down deep in the gear-box. His face was perplexed and angry. Sparrowhawk said nothing, till he said, "Will you take the oars now, lad. We're heading for the pier there by the stairs."

Hort Town, one of the Seven Great Ports of the Archipelago, rose from its noisy waterfront up the slopes of three steep hills in a jumble of colour. The houses were of clay plastered in red, orange, yellow, white; the roofs were of purplish-red tile; pendick-trees in flower made masses of dark red along the upper streets. Gaudy striped awnings stretched from roof to roof, shading narrow marketplaces. The quays were bright with sunlight; the streets running back from the waterfront were like dark slots full of shadows and people and noise.

When they had tied up the boat, Sparrowhawk stooped over as if to check the knot, beside Arren, and he said, "Arren, there are people in Wathort who know me pretty well; so watch me, that you may know me." When he straightened up there was no scar on his face. His hair was quite grey; his nose was thick and somewhat snub; and instead of a yew staff his own height, he carried a wand of ivory, which he tucked away inside his shirt. "Dost know me?" he said to Arren with a broad smile, and he spoke with the accent of Enlad. "Hast never seen thy nuncle before this?"

Arren had seen wizards at the court of Berila change their

faces when they mimed the *Deed of Morred*, and knew it was only illusion; he kept his wits about him, and was able to say, "Oh aye, nuncle Hawk!"

But, while the mage dickered with a harbour guardsman over the fee for docking and guarding the boat, Arren kept looking at him to make sure that he did know him. And as he looked, the transformation troubled him more, not less. It was too complete; this was not the Archmage at all, this was no wise guide and leader. . . . The guardsman's fee was high, and Sparrowhawk grumbled as he paid, and strode away with Arren, still grumbling. "A test of my patience," he said. "Pay that swag-bellied thief to guard my boat! when half a spell would do twice the job! Well, this is the price of disguise. . . . And I've forgot my proper speech, have I not, nevvy?"

They were walking up a crowded, smelly, gaudy street lined with shops, little more than booths, whose owners stood in the doorways among heaps and festoons of wares, loudly proclaiming the beauty and cheapness of their pots, hosiery, hats, spades, pins, purses, kettles, baskets, firehooks, knives, ropes, bolts, bedlinens, and every other kind of hardware and dry-goods. "Is it a fair?"

"Eh?" said the snub-nosed man, bending his grizzled head.

"Is it a fair, nuncle?"

"Fair? No, no. They keep it up all year round, here. Keep your fishcakes, mistress, I have breakfasted!" And Arren tried to shake off a man with a tray of little brass vases, who followed at his heels whining, "Buy, try, handsome young master, they won't fail you, breath as sweet as the roses of Numima, charming the women to you, try them, young sealord, young prince. . . ."

All at once Sparrowhawk was between Arren and the pedlar, saying, "What charms are these?"

"Not charms!" the man whined, shrinking away from him. "I sell no charms, seamaster! Only syrups to sweeten the breath after drink or hazia-root—only syrups, great prince!" He cowered right down onto the pavement stones, his tray of vases clinking and clattering, some of them tipping so that a drop of the sticky stuff inside oozed out, pink or purple, over the lip.

Sparrowhawk turned away without speaking, and went on with Arren. Soon the crowds thinned and the shops grew wretchedly poor, little kennels displaying as all their wares a handful of bent nails, a broken pestle and an old carding-comb. This poverty disgusted Arren less than the rest; in the rich end of the street he had felt choked, suffocated, by the pressure of things to be sold and voices screaming to him to buy, buy. And the pedlar's abjectness had shocked him. He thought of the cool, bright streets of his Northern town. No man in Berila, he thought, would have grovelled to a stranger like that. "These are a foul folk!" he said.

"This way, nevvy," was all his companion's answer. They turned aside into a passage between high, red, windowless housewalls, which ran along the hillside and through an archway garlanded with decaying banners, out again into the sunlight in a steep square, another marketplace, crowded with booths and stalls and swarming with people and flies.

Around the edges of the square a number of men and women were sitting or lying on their backs, motionless. Their mouths had a curious blackish look, as if they had been bruised, and around their lips flies swarmed and gathered in clusters like bunches of dried currants.

"So many," said Sparrowhawk's voice, low and hasty as if he too had got a shock; but when Arren looked at him there was the blunt bland face of the hearty trader Hawk, showing no concern.

"What's wrong with those people?"

"Hazia. It soothes and numbs, letting the body be free of the mind. And the mind roams free. But when it returns to the body it needs more hazia. . . . And the craving grows; and the life is short, for the stuff is poison. First there is a trembling, and later paralysis, and then death."

Arren looked at a woman sitting with her back to a sun-warmed wall; she had raised her hand as if to brush away the flies from her face, but the hand made a jerky, circular motion in the air, as if she had quite forgotten about it and it was moved only by the repeated surging of a palsy or shaking in the muscles. The gesture was like an incantation emptied of all intention, a spell without meaning.

Hawk was looking at her too, expressionless. "Come on!" he said.

He led on across the marketplace to an awning-shaded booth. Stripes of sunlight coloured green, orange, lemon, crimson, azure, fell across the cloths and shawls and woven belts displayed, and danced multitudinous in the tiny mirrors that bedecked the high, feathered headdress of the woman who sold the stuff. She was big, and she chanted in a big voice, "Silks, satins, canvases, furs, felts, woollens, fleecefells of Gont, gauzes of Sowl, silks of Lorbanery! Hey, you Northern men, take off your duffle-coats, don't you see the sun's out? How's this to take home to a girl in far Havnor? Look at it, silk of the South, fine as the mayfly's wing!" She had flipped open with deft hands a bolt of gauzy silk, pink shot with threads of silver.

"Nay, mistress, we're not wed to queens," said Hawk, and the woman's voice rose to a blare: "So what do you dress your womenfolk in, burlap? sailcloth? Misers that won't buy a bit of silk for a poor woman freezing in the everlasting Northern snow! How's this then, a Gontish fleecefell, to help you keep her warm on winter nights!" She flung out over the counter-board a great cream and brown square, woven of the silky hair of the goats of the northeastern isles. The pretended trader put out his hand and felt it; and he smiled.

"Aye, you're a Gontishman?" said the blaring voice, and the headdress nodding sent a thousand coloured dots spinning over the canopy and the cloth.

"This is Andradean work; see? There's but four warpstrings to the finger's width. Gont uses six or more. But tell me why you've turned from working magic to selling fripperies. When I was here years since I saw you pulling flames out of men's ears, and then you made the flames turn into birds and golden bells, and that was a finer trade than this one."

"It was no trade at all," the big woman said, and for a moment Arren was aware of her eyes, hard and steady as agates, looking at him and Hawk from out of the glitter and restlessness of her nodding feathers and flashing mirrors.

"It was pretty, that pulling fire out of ears," said Hawk in a dour but simple-minded tone. "I thought to show it to my nevvy."

"Well now look you," said the woman less harshly, leaning her broad brown arms and heavy bosom on the counter. "We don't do those tricks any more. People don't want 'em. They've seen through 'em. These mirrors now, I see you remember my mirrors," and she tossed her head so that the reflected dots of coloured light whirled dizzily about them, "well, you can puzzle a man's mind with the flashing of the mirrors, and with words, and with other tricks I won't tell you, till he thinks he sees what he don't see, what isn't there. Like the flames and golden bells, or the suits of clothes I used to deck sailormen in, cloth of gold with diamonds like apricots, and off they'd swagger like the King of All the Isles. . . . But it was tricks, fooleries. You can fool men. They're like chickens charmed by a snake, by a finger held before 'em. Men are like chickens. But then in the end they know they've been fooled and fuddled, and they get angry, and lose their pleasure in such things. So I turned to this trade, and maybe all the silks aren't silks nor all the fleeces Gontish, but all the same they'll wear—they'll wear!

They're real, and not mere lies and air, like the suits of cloth of gold."

"Well, well," said Hawk, "then there's none left in all Hort Town to pull fire out of ears, or do any magic like they did?"

At his last words the woman frowned; she straightened up and began to fold the fleecefell carefully. "Those who want lies and visions chew hazia," she said. "Talk to them if you like!" She nodded to the unmoving figures around the square.

"But there were sorcerers, they that charmed the winds for seamen and put spells of fortune on their cargoes. Are they all turned to other trades?"

But she in sudden fury came blaring in over his words, "There's a sorcerer if you want one, a great one, a wizard with a staff and all—see him there? He sailed with Egre himself, making winds and finding fat galleys, so he said, but it was all lies, and Captain Egre gave him his just reward at last, he cut his right hand off. And there he sits now, see him, with his mouth full of hazia and his belly full of air. Air and lies! Air and lies! That's all there is to your magic, Seacaptain Goat!"

"Well, well, mistress," said Hawk with obdurate mildness, "I was only asking." She turned her broad back with a great dazzle of whirling mirror-dots, and he ambled off, Arren beside him.

His amble was purposeful. It brought them near the man she had pointed out. He sat propped against a wall, staring at nothing; the dark, bearded face had been very handsome once. The wrinkled wrist-stump lay on the pavement stones in the hot, bright sunlight, shameful.

There was some commotion among the booths behind them, but Arren found it hard to look away from the man; a loathing fascination held him. "Was he really a wizard?" he asked very low.

"He may be the one called Hare, who was weatherworker for

the pirate Egre. They were famous thieves—Here, stand clear, Arren!" A man running full tilt out from among the booths nearly slammed into them both. Another came trotting by, struggling under the weight of a great folding tray loaded with cords and braids and laces. A booth collapsed with a crash; awnings were being pushed over or taken down hurriedly; knots of people shoved and wrestled through the market-place, voices rose in shouts and screams. Above them all rang the blaring yell of the woman with the headdress of mirrors; Arren glimpsed her wielding some kind of pole or stick against a bunch of men, fending them off with great sweeps like a swordsman at bay. Whether it was a quarrel that had spread and become a riot, or an attack by a gang of thieves, or a fight between two rival lots of pedlars, there was no telling; people rushed by with armfuls of goods that could be loot or their own property saved from looting, there were knife-fights, fist-fights, and brawls all over the square. "That way," said Arren, pointing to a side street that led out of the square near them, and started for it, for it was clear that they had better get out at once; but his companion caught his arm. Arren looked back, and saw that the man Hare was struggling to his feet. When he got himself erect he stood swaying a moment, and then without a look around him set off around the edge of the square, trailing his single hand along the house-walls as if to guide or support himself. "Keep him in sight," Sparrowhawk said, and they set off following. No one molested them or the man they followed, and in a minute they were out of the market-square, going downhill in the silence of a narrow, twisting street.

Overhead the attics of the houses almost met across the street, cutting out light; underfoot the stones were slippery with water and refuse. Hare went along at a good pace, though he kept trailing his hand along the walls like a blind man. They had to keep pretty close behind him lest they lose him at a cross-street. The excitement of the chase came into Arren suddenly; his senses were all alert, as they were during a stag-hunt in the forests of Enlad; he saw vividly each face they passed, and breathed in the sweet stink of the city, a smell of garbage, incense, carrion and flowers. As they threaded their way across a broad, crowded street he heard a drum beat, and caught a glimpse of a line of naked men and women, chained each to the next by wrist and waist, matted hair hanging over their faces: one glimpse and they were gone, as he dodged after Hare down a flight of steps and out into a narrow square, empty but for a few women gossiping at the fountain.

There Sparrowhawk caught up with Hare and set a hand on his shoulder, at which Hare cringed as if scalded, wincing away, and backed into the shelter of a massive doorway. There he stood shivering, and stared at them with the unseeing eyes of the hunted.

"Are you called Hare?" asked Sparrowhawk, and he spoke in his own voice, which was harsh in quality, but gentle in intonation. The man said nothing, seeming not to heed or not to hear. "I want something of you," Sparrowhawk said. Again no response. "I'll pay for it."

A slow reaction: "Ivory or gold?"

"Gold."

"How much?"

"The wizard knows the spell's worth."

Hare's face flinched and changed, coming alive for an instant, so quickly that it seemed to flicker, then clouding again into blankness. "That's all gone," he said, "all gone." A coughing fit bent him over; he spat black. When he straightened up he stood passive, shivering, seeming to have forgotten what they were talking about.

Again Arren watched him in fascination. The angle in which he stood was formed by two giant figures flanking a doorway, statues whose necks were bowed under the weight of a pediment and whose knot-muscled bodies emerged only partially from the wall, as if they had tried to struggle out of stone into life and had failed partway. The door they guarded was rotten on its hinges; the house, once a palace, was derelict. The gloomy, bulging faces of the giants were chipped and lichen-grown. Between these ponderous figures the man called Hare stood slack and fragile, his eyes as dark as the windows of the empty house. He lifted up his maimed arm between himself and Sparrowhawk and whined, "Spare a little for a poor cripple, master. . . ."

The mage scowled as if in pain, or shame; Arren felt he had seen his true face for a moment under the disguise. He put his hand again on Hare's shoulder and said a few words, softly, in the wizardly tongue that Arren did not understand.

But Hare understood. He clutched at Sparrowhawk with his one hand, and stammered, "You can still speak—speak—Come with me, come——"

The mage glanced at Arren, then nodded.

They went down by steep streets into one of the valleys between Hort Town's three hills. The ways became narrower, darker, quieter as they descended. The sky was a pale strip between the overhanging eaves, and the house walls to either hand were dank. At the bottom of the gorge a stream ran, stinking like an open sewer; between arched bridges houses crowded along its banks, and into the dark doorway of one of these houses Hare turned aside, vanishing like a candle blown out. They followed him.

The unlit stairs creaked and swayed under their feet. At the head of the stairs Hare pushed open a door, and they could see where they were: an empty room with a straw-stuffed mattress in one corner and one unglazed, shuttered window that let in a little dusty light.

Hare turned to face Sparrowhawk and caught at his arm again. His lips worked. He said at last, stammering, "Dragon . . . dragon . . ."

Sparrowhawk returned his look steadily, saying nothing.

"I cannot speak," Hare said, and he let go his hold on Sparrowhawk's arm and crouched down on the empty floor, weeping.

The mage knelt by him and spoke to him softly in the Old Speech. Arren stood by the shut door, his hand on his knife-hilt. The grey light and the dusty room, the two kneeling figures, the soft strange sound of the mage's voice speaking the language of the dragons, all came together as does a dream, having no relation to what happens outside it or to time passing.

Slowly Hare stood up. He dusted his knees with his single hand, and hid the maimed arm behind his back. He looked around him, looked at Arren; he was seeing what he looked at, now. He turned away presently and sat down on his mattress. Arren remained standing, on guard; but, with the simplicity of one whose childhood was totally unfurnished, Sparrowhawk sat down cross-legged on the bare floor. "Tell me how you lost your craft, and the language of your craft," he said.

Hare did not answer for a while. He began to beat his mutilated arm against his thigh in a restless, jerky way, and at last he said, forcing the words out in bursts, "They cut off my hand. I can't weave the spells. They cut off my hand. The blood ran out, ran dry."

"But that was after you'd lost your power, Hare, or else they could not have done it."

"Power . . ."

"Power over the winds, and the waves, and men. You called them by their names and they obeyed you."

"Yes. I remember being alive," the man said in a soft hoarse voice. "And I knew the words, and the names. . . ."

"Are you dead now?"

"No. Alive. Alive. Only once I was a dragon. . . . I'm not dead. I sleep sometimes. Sleep comes very close to death,

55

everyone knows that. The dead walk in dreams, everyone knows that. They come to you alive, and they say things. They walk out of death into the dreams. There's a way. And if you go on far enough there's a way back all the way. All the way. You can find it if you know where to look. And if you're willing to pay the price."

"What price is that?" Sparrowhawk's voice floated on the dim air like the shadow of a falling leaf.

"Life—what else? What can you buy life with, but life?" Hare rocked back and forth on his pallet, a cunning, uncanny brightness in his eyes. "You see," he said, "they can cut off my hand. They can cut off my head. It doesn't matter. I can find the way back. I know where to look. Only men of power can go there."

"Wizards, you mean?"

"Yes." Hare hesitated, seeming to attempt the word several times; he could not say it. "Men of power," he repeated. "And they must—and they must give it up. Pay."

Then he fell sullen, as if the word "pay" had at last roused associations, and he had realised that he was giving information away instead of selling it. Nothing more could be got from him, not even the hints and stammers about "a way back" which Sparrowhawk seemed to find meaningful, and soon enough the mage stood up. "Well, half answers beat no answer," he said, "and the same with payment," and, deft as a conjuror, he flipped a gold piece onto the pallet in front of Hare.

Hare picked it up. He looked at it, and Sparrowhawk, and Arren, with jerky movements of his head. "Wait," he stammered. As soon as the situation changed he lost his grip of it, and now groped miserably after what he wanted to say. "Tonight," he said at last. "Wait. Tonight. I have hazia."

"I don't need it."

"To show you—To show you the way. Tonight. I'll take you. I'll show you. You can get there, because you . . .

you're . . ." He groped for the word until Sparrowhawk said, "I am a wizard."

"Yes! So we can—we can get there. To the way. When I dream. In the dream. See? I'll take you. You'll go with me, to the . . . to the way."

Sparrowhawk stood, solid and pondering, in the middle of the dim room. "Maybe," he said at last. "If we come, we'll be here by dark." Then he turned to Arren, who opened the door at once, eager to be gone.

The dank overshadowed street seemed bright as a garden after Hare's room. They struck out for the upper city by the shortest way, a steep stairway of stone between ivy-grown housewalls. Arren breathed in and out like a sea-lion—"Ugh!— Are you going back there?"

"Well, I will, if I can't get the same information from a less risky source. He's likely to set an ambush for us."

"But aren't you defended against thieves and so on?"

"Defended?" said Sparrowhawk. "What do you mean? D'you think I go about wrapped up in spells like an old woman afraid of the rheumatism? I haven't the time for it. I hide my face to hide our quest; that's all. We can look out for each other. But the fact is we're not going to be able to keep out of danger on this journey."

"Of course not," Arren said stiffly, angry, angered in his pride. "I did not seek to do so."

"That's just as well," the mage said, inflexible, and yet with a kind of good humour that appeased Arren's temper. Indeed, he was startled by his own anger; he had never thought to speak thus to the Archmage. But then, this was and was not the Archmage, this Hawk with the snub nose and square, ill-shaven cheeks, whose voice was sometimes one man's voice and sometimes another's: a stranger, unreliable.

"Does it make sense, what he told you?" Arren asked, for he did not look forward to going back to that dim room above the

57

stinking river. "All that fibblefabble about being alive and dead and coming back with his head cut off?"

"I don't know if it makes sense. I wanted to talk with a wizard who has lost his power. He says that he hasn't lost it but given it—traded it. For what? Life for life, he said. Power for power. No, I don't understand him, but he is worth listening to."

Sparrowhawk's steady reasonableness shamed Arren further. He felt himself petulant and nervous, like a child. Hare had fascinated him, but now that the fascination was broken he felt a sick disgust, as if he had eaten something vile. He resolved not to speak again until he had controlled his temper. Next moment he missed his step on the worn, slick stairs, slipped, recovered himself scraping his hands on the stones. "Oh curse this filthy town!" he broke out in rage. And the mage replied dryly, "No need to, I think."

There was indeed something wrong about Hort Town, wrong in the very air, so that one might think seriously that it lay under a curse; and yet this was not a presence of any quality but rather an absence, a weakening of all qualities, like a sickness that soon infected the spirit of any visitor. Even the warmth of the afternoon sun was sickly, too heavy a heat for March. The squares and streets bustled with activity and business, but there was neither order nor prosperity. Goods were poor, prices high, and the markets were unsafe for vendors and buyers alike, being full of thieves and roaming gangs. Not many women were on the streets, and then mostly in groups. It was a city without law or governance. Talking with people, Arren and Sparrowhawk soon learned that there was in fact no council or mayor or lord left in Hort Town. Some of those who had used to rule the city had died, and some had resigned, and some had been assassinated; various chiefs lorded it over various quarters of the city, the harbour guardsmen ran the port and lined their pockets, and so on. There was no centre left to the city. The people, for all their restless activity, seemed purposeless.

Craftsmen seemed to lack the will to work well; even the robbers robbed because it was all they knew how to do. All the brawl and brightness of a great port-city was there, on the surface, but all about the edges of it sat the hazia-eaters, motionless. And under the surface things did not seem entirely real, not even the faces, the sounds, the smells. They would fade, from time to time during that long, warm afternoon while Sparrowhawk and Arren walked the streets and talked with this person and that. They would fade quite away, the striped awnings, the dirty cobbles, the coloured walls, and all vividness of being would be gone, leaving the city a dream city, empty and dreary in the hazy sunlight.

Only at the top of the town where they went to rest a while in late afternoon did this sickly mood of daydream break for a while. "This is not a town for luck," Sparrowhawk had said some hours ago, and now after hours of aimless wandering and fruitless conversations with strangers, he looked tired and grim. His disguise was wearing a little thin; a certain hardness and darkness could be seen through the bluff sea-trader's face. Arren had never been able to shake off the morning's irrit-ability. They sat down on the coarse turf of the hilltop under the eaves of a grove of pendick trees, dark-leaved and budded thickly with red buds, some open. From there they saw nothing of the city but its tile roofs multitudinously scaling downward to the sea. The bay opened its arms wide, slate blue beneath the spring haze, reaching on to the edge of air. No lines were drawn, no boundaries. They sat gazing at that immense blue space. Arren's mind cleared, opening out to meet and celebrate the world.

When they went to drink from a little stream nearby, running clear over brown rocks from its spring in some princely garden on the hill behind them, he drank deep, and doused his head right under the cold water. Then he got up and declaimed the lines from the *Deed of Morred*,

Praised are the Fountains of Shelieth, the silver harp
  of the waters,
But blest in my name forever this stream that
  stanched my thirst!

Sparrowhawk laughed at him, and he also laughed. He shook his head like a dog, and the bright spray flew out fine in the last gold sunlight.

They had to leave the grove and go down into the streets again, and when they had made their supper at a stall that sold greasy fishcakes, night was getting heavy in the air. Darkness came fast in the narrow streets. "We'd better go, lad," said Sparrowhawk, and Arren said, "To the boat?" but knew it was not to the boat but to the house above the river and the empty, dusty, terrible room.

Hare was waiting for them in the doorway.

He lighted an oil lamp to show them up the black stairs. Its tiny flame trembled continually as he held it, throwing vast, quick shadows up the walls.

He had got another sack of straw for his visitors to sit on, but Arren took his place on the bare floor by the door. The door opened outward, and to guard it he should have sat himself down outside it: but that pitchblack hall was more than he could stand, and he wanted to keep an eye on Hare. Sparrowhawk's attention, and perhaps his powers, were going to be turned on what Hare had to tell him, or show him; it was up to Arren to keep alert for trickery.

Hare held himself straighter, and trembled less; he had cleaned his mouth and teeth; he spoke sanely enough, at first, though with excitement. His eyes in the lamplight were so dark that they seemed, like the eyes of animals, to show no whites. He disputed earnestly with Sparrowhawk, urging him to eat hazia. "I want to take you, take you with me. We've got to go the same way. Before long I'll be going whether you're ready or not. You must have the hazia to follow me."

"I think I can follow you."

"Not where I'm going. This isn't . . . spell-casting." He seemed unable to say the words 'wizard' or 'wizardry'. "I know you can get to the—the place, you know, the wall. But it isn't there. It's a different way."

"If you go, I can follow."

Hare shook his head. His handsome, ruined face was flushed; he glanced over at Arren often, including him, though he spoke only to Sparrowhawk. "Look: there are two kinds of man, aren't there? Our kind, and the rest. The . . . the dragons, and the others. People without power are only half alive. They don't count. They don't know what they dream, they're afraid of the dark. But the others, the lords of men, aren't afraid to go into the dark. We have strength."

"So long as we know the names of things."

"But names don't matter there—that's the point, that's the point! It isn't what you do, what you know, that you need. Spells are no good. You have to forget all that, to let it go. That's where eating hazia helps, you forget the names, you let the forms of things go, you go straight to the reality. I'm going to be going pretty soon now, if you want to find out where you ought to do as I say. I say as he does. You must be a lord of men to be a lord of life. You have to find the secret. I could tell you its name but what's a name? A name isn't real, the real, the real forever. Dragons can't go there. Dragons die. They all die. I took so much tonight you'll never catch me. Not a patch on me. Where I get lost you can lead me. Remember what the secret is? Remember? No death. No death—no! No sweaty bed and rotting coffin, no more, never. The blood dries up like the dry river and it's gone. No fear. No death. The names are gone and the words and the fear, gone. Show me where I get lost, show me, lord. . . ."

So he went on, in a choked rapture of words that was like the chanting of a spell and yet made no spell, no whole, no sense. Arren listened, listened, striving to understand. If only he could understand! Sparrowhawk should do as he said and take the drug, this once, so that he could find out what Hare was talking about, the mystery that he would not or could not speak. Why else were they here? But then (Arren looked from Hare's ecstatic face to the other profile) perhaps the mage understood already. . . . Hard as rock, that profile. Where was the snub nose, the bland look? Hawk the sea-trader was gone, forgotten. It was the mage, the Archmage, who sat there.

Hare's voice now was a crooning mumble, and he rocked his body as he sat crosslegged. His face had grown haggard and his mouth slack. Facing him, in the tiny, steady light of the oil lamp set on the floor between them, the other never spoke, but he had reached out and taken Hare's hand, holding him. Arren had not seen him reach out. There were gaps in the order of events, gaps of non-existence—drowsiness, it must be. Surely some hours had passed, it might be near midnight. If he slept, would he too be able to follow Hare into his dream, and come to the place, the secret way? Perhaps he could. It seemed quite possible now. But he was to guard the door. He and Sparrow-hawk had scarcely spoken of it but both were aware that in having them come back at night Hare might have planned some ambush; he had been a pirate, he knew robbers. They had said nothing, but Arren knew that he was to stand guard, for while the mage made this strange journey of the spirit he would be defenceless. But like a fool he had left his sword on board the boat, and how much good would his knife be if that door swung suddenly open behind him? But that would not happen: he could listen, and hear. Hare was not speaking any more, both men were utterly silent, the whole house was silent. Nobody could come up those swaying stairs without some noise. He could speak, if he heard a noise: shout aloud, and the trance would break, and Sparrowhawk would turn and defend himself

and Arren with all the vengeful lightning of a wizard's rage . . . .
When Arren had sat down at the door Sparrowhawk had looked
at him, only a glance, approval: approval and trust. He was
the guard. There was no danger if he kept on guard. But it
was hard, hard to keep watching those two faces, the little
pearl of the lamp-flame between them on the floor, both
silent now, both still, their eyes open but not seeing the light
or the dusty room, not seeing the world, but some other world
of dream or death . . . to watch them, and not to try to follow
them. . . .

There, in the vast, dry darkness, there one stood beckoning.
Come, he said, the tall lord of shadows. In his hand he held
a tiny flame no larger than a pearl, held it out to Arren, offering
life. Slowly Arren took one step towards him, following.

4   *Magelight*

Dry, his mouth was dry. There was the taste of dust in his mouth. His lips were covered with dust.

Without lifting his head from the floor he watched the shadow-play. There were the big shadows that moved and stooped, swelled and shrank, and fainter ones that ran around the walls and ceiling swiftly, mocking them. There was a shadow in the corner, and a shadow on the floor, and neither of these moved.

The back of his head began to hurt. At the same time, what he saw came clear to his mind, in one flash, frozen in an instant: Hare slumped in a corner with his head on his knees, Sparrow-hawk sprawled on his back, a man kneeling over Sparrowhawk, another tossing gold pieces into a bag, a third standing watching. The third man held a lantern in one hand and a dagger in the other, Arren's dagger.

If they talked he did not hear them. He heard only his own thoughts, which told him immediately and unhesitatingly what to do. He obeyed them at once. He crawled forward very slowly a couple of feet, darted out his left hand and grabbed the bag of loot, leapt to his feet, and made for the stairs with a hoarse yell. He plunged downstairs in the blind dark without missing a step, without even feeling them under his feet, as if he were flying.

He broke out onto the street and ran fullspeed into the dark.

The houses were black hulks against stars. Starlight gleamed faintly on the river to his right, and though he could not see where the streets led, he could make out street-crossings, and so turn and double on his track. They had followed him, he could hear them behind him, not very far behind. They were unshod, and their panting breathing was louder than their footfalls. He would have laughed if he had had time; he knew at last what it was like to be the hunted instead of the hunter, the leader of the chase, the quarry. It was to be alone, and to be free. He swerved to the right and dodged stooping across a high-parapeted bridge, slipped into a sidestreet, around a corner, back to the riverside and along it for a way, across another bridge. His shoes were loud on the cobblestones, the only sound in all the city; he paused at the bridge abutment to unlace them, but the strings were knotted, and the hunt had not lost him. The lantern glittered a second across the river, the soft, heavy, running feet came on. He could not get away from them, he could only outrun them, keep going, keep ahead, and get them away from the dusty room, far away. . . . They had stripped his coat off him, along with his dagger, and he was in shirt-sleeves, light and hot, his head swimming and the pain in the back of his skull pointing and pointing with each stride, and he ran, and he ran. . . . The bag hindered him. He flung it down suddenly, a loose gold piece flying out and striking the stones with a clear ring. "Here's your money!" he yelled, his voice hoarse and gasping. He ran on. And all at once the street ended. No cross streets, no stars before him, a dead end. Without pausing he turned back and ran at his pursuers. The lantern swung wild in his eyes, and he yelled defiance as he came at them.

There was a lantern swinging back and forth before him, a

faint spot of light in a great moving greyness. He watched it for a long time. It grew fainter, and at last a shadow passed before it, and when the shadow went on the light was gone. He grieved for it a little; or perhaps he was grieving for himself, because he knew he must wake up now.

The lantern, dead, still swung against the mast to which it was fixed. All around, the sea brightened with the coming sun. A drum beat. Oars creaked heavily, regularly; the wood of the ship cried and creaked in a hundred little voices; a man up in the prow called something to the sailors behind him. The men chained with Arren in the after hold were all silent. Each wore an iron band around his waist, and manacles on his wrists, and both these bonds were linked by a short heavy chain to the bonds of the next man; the belt of iron was also chained to a bolt in the deck, so that the man could sit, or crouch, but could not stand. They were too close together to lie down, jammed together in the small cargo-hold. Arren was in the forward port corner. If he lifted his head high his eyes were on a level with the decking between hold and rail, a couple of feet wide.

He did not remember much of last night past the chase and the dead-end street. He had fought, and been knocked down and trussed up, and carried somewhere. A man with a strange whispering voice had spoken; there had been a place like a smithy, a forge-fire leaping red . . . he could not recall it. He knew, though, that this was a slave-ship, and that he had been taken to be sold.

It did not mean much to him. He was too thirsty. His body ached and his head hurt. When the sun rose the light sent lances of pain into his eyes.

Along in mid morning they were given a quarter of bread each and a long drink from a leather flask, held to their lips by a man with a sharp, hard face. His neck was clasped by a broad, gold-studded leather band like a dog's collar, and when Arren heard him speak he recognised the weak, strange, whistling voice.

Drink and food eased his bodily wretchedness for a while, and cleared his head. He looked for the first time at the faces of his fellow slaves, three in his row and four close behind. Some sat with their heads on their raised knees; one was slumped over, sick or drugged. The one next to Arren was a fellow of twenty or so with a broad, flat face. "Where are they taking us?" Arren said to him.

The fellow looked at him—their faces were not a foot apart —and grinned, shrugging, and Arren thought he meant he did not know; but then he jerked his manacled arms as if to gesture, and opened his still grinning mouth wide to show, where the tongue should be, only a black root.

"It'll be Showl," said one behind Arren, and another, "Or the Market at Amrun," and then the man with the collar, who seemed to be everywhere on the ship, was bending above the hold hissing, "Be still if you don't want to be sharkbait," and all of them were still.

Arren tried to imagine these places, Showl, the Market of Amrun. They sold slaves there. They stood them out in front of the buyers, no doubt, like oxen or rams for sale in Berila Marketplace. He would stand there wearing chains. Somebody would buy him and lead him home, and they would give him an order; and he would refuse to obey. Or obey, and try to escape. And he would be killed, one way or the other. It was not that his soul rebelled at the thought of slavery, he was much too sick and bewildered for that, it was simply that he knew he could not do it, that within a week or two he would die or be killed. Though he saw and accepted this as a fact it frightened him, so that he stopped trying to think ahead. He stared down at the foul black planking of the hold between his feet, and felt the heat of the sun on his naked shoulders, and felt the thirst drying out his mouth and narrowing his throat again.

The sun sank, night came on clear and cold. The sharp stars came out. The drum beat like a slow heart, keeping the oar-stroke, for there was no breath of wind. Now the cold became the greatest misery. Arren's back gained a little warmth from the cramped legs of the man behind him, and his left side from the mute beside him, who sat hunched up, humming a grunting rhythm all on one note. The rowers changed shift, the drum beat again. Arren had longed for the darkness, but he could not sleep; his bones ached, and he could not change position. He sat aching, shivering, parched, staring up at the stars, which jerked across the sky with every stroke the oarsmen took, slid to their places and were still, jerked again, slid, paused. . . .

The man with the collar and another stood between the after hold and the mast; the little swinging lantern on the mast sent gleams between them and silhouetted their heads and shoulders. "Fog, you pig's bladder," said the weak hateful voice of the man with the collar, "what's a fog doing in the Southing Straits this time of year? Curse the luck!"

The drum beat. The stars jerked, slid, paused. Beside Arren the tongueless man shuddered all at once and raising his head let out a nightmare scream, a terrible, formless noise. "Quiet there!" roared the second man by the mast. The mute shuddered again and was silent, munching with his jaws.

Stealthily the stars slid forward into nothingness.

The mast wavered and vanished. A cold grey blanket seemed to drop over Arren's back. The drum faltered, then resumed its beat, but slower.

"Thick as curdled milk," said the hoarse voice somewhere above Arren. "Keep up the stroke there! there's no shoals for twenty miles!" A horny, scarred foot appeared out of the fog, paused an instant close to Arren's face, then with one step vanished.

In the fog there was no sense of forward motion, only of

swaying, and the tug of the oars. The throb of the stroke-drum was muffled. It was clammy cold. The mist condensing in Arren's hair ran down into his eyes; he tried to catch the drops with his tongue, and breathed the damp air with open mouth, trying to assuage his thirst. But his teeth chattered. The cold metal of a chain swung against his thigh, and burned like fire where it touched. The drum beat, and beat, and ceased.

It was silent.

"Keep the beat! What's amiss?" roared the hoarse, whistling voice from the prow. No answer came.

The ship rolled a little on the quiet sea. Beyond the dim rails was nothing: blank. Something grated against the ship's side. The noise was loud in that dead, weird silence and darkness. "We're aground," one of the prisoners whispered, but the silence closed in on his voice.

The fog grew bright, as if a light were blooming in it. Arren saw the heads of the men chained by him clearly, the tiny moisture-drops shining in their hair. Again the ship swayed, and he strained as far up as his chains would let him, stretching his neck, to see forward in the ship. The fog glowed over the deck like the moon behind thin cloud, cold and radiant. The oarsmen sat like carved statues. Crewmen stood in the waist of the ship, their eyes shining a little. Alone on the port side stood a man, and it was from him that the light came, from the face, and hands, and staff that burned like molten silver.

At the feet of the radiant man a dark shape was crouched.

Arren tried to speak, and could not. Clothed in that majesty of light, the Archmage came to him, and knelt down on the deck. Arren felt the touch of his hand, and heard his voice. He felt the bonds on his wrists and body give way; all through the hold there was a rattling of chains. But no man moved; only Arren tried to stand, but he could not, being cramped with long immobility. The Archmage's strong grip was on his arm, and with that help he crawled up out of the cargo-hold, and huddled on the deck.

The Archmage strode away from him, and the misty splendour glowed on the unmoving faces of the oarsmen. He halted by the man who had crouched down by the port rail.

"I do not punish," said the hard, clear voice, cold as the cold magelight in the fog. "But in the cause of justice, Egre, I take this much upon myself: I bid your voice be dumb until the day you find a word worth speaking."

He came back to Arren and helped him to get to his feet. "Come on now, lad," he said, and with his help Arren managed to hobble forward, and half-scramble, half-fall down into the boat that rocked there below the ship's side: *Lookfar*, her sail like a moth's wing in the fog.

In the same silence and dead calm the light died away, and the boat turned and slipped from the ship's side. Almost at once the galley, the dim mast-lantern, the immobile oarsmen, the hulking black side, were gone. Arren thought he heard voices break out in cries, but the sound was thin and soon lost. A little longer, and the fog began to thin and tatter, blowing by in the dark. They came out under the stars, and silent as a moth *Lookfar* fled through the clear night over the sea.

Sparrowhawk had covered Arren with blankets, and given him water; he sat with his hand on the boy's shoulder when he fell suddenly to weeping. He said nothing, but there was a gentleness, a steadiness, in the touch of his hand. Comfort came slowly into Arren: warmth, the soft motion of the boat, heart's ease.

He looked up at his companion. No unearthly radiance clung to the dark face. He could barely see him, against the stars.

The boat fled on, charm-guided. Waves whispered as if in surprise along her sides.

"Who is the man with the collar?"

"Lie still. A sea-robber, Egre. He wears that collar to hide a scar where his throat was slit once. It seems his trade has sunk from piracy to slaving. But he took the bear's cub this time." There was a slight ring of satisfaction in the dry, quiet voice.

"How did you find me?"

"Wizardry, bribery. . . . I wasted time. I did not like to let it be known that the Archmage and Warden of Roke was ferreting about the slums of Hort Town. I wish still I could have kept up my disguise. But I had to track down this man and that man, and when at last I found that the slaver had sailed before daybreak, I lost my temper. I took *Lookfar* and spoke the wind into her sail, in the dead calm of the day, and glued the oars of every ship in that bay fast into the oar-locks—for a while—How they'll explain that, if wizardry's all lies and air, is their problem. But in my haste and anger I missed and overpassed Egre's ship, which had gone east of south to miss the shoals. Ill done was all I did this day. There is no luck in Hort Town. . . . Well, I made a spell of finding at last, and so came on the ship in the darkness. Should you not sleep now?"

"I'm all right, I feel much better." A light fever had replaced Arren's chill, and he did indeed feel well, his body languid but his mind racing lightly from one thing to another. "How soon did you wake up? What happened to Hare?"

"I woke with daylight; and lucky I have a hard head; there's a lump and a cut like a split cucumber behind my ear. I left Hare in the drug-sleep."

"I failed my guard—"

"But not by falling asleep."

"No." Arren hesitated. "It was—I was—"

"You were ahead of me; I saw you," Sparrowhawk said strangely. "And so they crept in and tapped us on the head like lambs at the shambles, took gold, good clothes, and the saleable slave, and left. It was you they were after, lad. You'd fetch the price of a farm in Amrun Market."

"They didn't tap me hard enough. I woke up. I did give them a run. I spilt their loot all over the street, too, before they cornered me." Arren's eyes glittered.

"You woke while they were there—and ran? Why?"

"To get them away from you." The surprise in Sparrowhawk's voice suddenly struck Arren's pride, and he added fiercely, "I thought it was you they were after. I thought they might kill you. I grabbed their bag so they'd follow me, and shouted out, and ran. And they did follow me."

"Aye—they would!" That was all Sparrowhawk said, no word of praise, though he sat and thought a while. Then he said, "Did it not occur to you I might be dead already?"

"No."

"Murder first and rob after, is the safer course."

"I didn't think of that. I only thought of getting them away from you."

"Why?"

"Because you might be able to defend us, to get us both out of it, if you had time to wake up. Or get yourself out of it, anyway. I was on guard and I failed my guard. I tried to make up for it. You are the one I was guarding. You are the one that matters. I'm along to guard, or whatever you need—it's you who'll lead us, who can get to wherever it is we must go, and put right what's gone wrong."

"Is it?" said the mage. "I thought so myself, until last night. I thought I had a follower, but I followed you, my lad." His voice was cool and perhaps a little ironic. Arren did not know what to say. He was indeed completely confused. He had thought that his fault of falling into sleep or trance on guard could scarcely be atoned by his feat of drawing off the robbers from Sparrowhawk: it now appeared that the latter had been a silly act, whereas going into trance at the wrong moment had been wonderfully clever.

"I am sorry, my lord," he said at last, his lips rather stiff and the need to cry not easily controlled again, "that I failed you. And you have saved my life—"

"And you mine, maybe," said the mage harshly. "Who knows? They might have slit my throat when they were done. No more of that, Arren. I am glad you are with me."

He went to their stores-box then, and lit their little charcoal stove, and busied himself with something. Arren lay and watched the stars, and his emotions cooled and his mind ceased racing. And he saw then that what he had done, and what he had not done, was not going to receive judgment from Sparrowhawk. He had done it; Sparrowhawk accepted it as done. "I do not punish," he had said, cold-voiced, to Egre. Neither did he reward. But he had come for Arren in all haste across the sea, unleashing the power of his wizardry for his sake; and he would do so again. He was to be depended on.

He was worth all the love Arren had for him, and all the trust. For the fact was that he trusted Arren. What Arren did, was right.

He came back now, handing Arren a cup of steaming hot wine. "Maybe that'll put you to sleep. Take care, it'll scald your tongue."

"Where did the wine come from? I never saw a wineskin aboard—"

"There's more in *Lookfar* than meets the eye," Sparrowhawk said, sitting down again beside him, and Arren heard him laugh, briefly and almost silently, in the dark.

Arren sat up to drink the wine. It was very good, refreshing body and spirit. He said, "Where are we going now?"

"Westward."

"Where did you go with Hare?"

"Into the darkness. I never lost him, but he was lost. He wandered on the outer borders, in the endless barrens of delirium and nightmare. His soul piped like a bird in those dreary places, like a seagull crying far from the sea. He is no guide. He has always been lost. For all his craft in sorcery he has never seen the way before him, seeing only himself."

Arren did not understand all of this; nor did he want to understand it, now. He had been drawn a little way into that 'darkness' of which wizards spoke, and he did not want to remember it; it was nothing to do with him. Indeed he did not want to sleep, lest he see it again in dream, and see that dark figure, a shadow holding out a pearl, whispering, "Come."

"My lord," he said, his mind veering away rapidly to another subject, "why—"

"Sleep!" said Sparrowhawk with mild exasperation.

"I can't sleep, my lord. I wondered why you didn't free the other slaves."

"I did. I left none bound on that ship."

"But Egre's men had weapons. If you had bound *them*—"

"Aye, if I had bound them? There were but six. The oarsmen were chained slaves, like you. Egre and his men may be dead by now, or chained by the others to be sold as slaves; but I left them free to fight, or bargain. I am no slave-taker."

"But you knew them to be evil men—"

"Was I to join them therefore? To let their acts rule my own? I will not make their choices for them, nor will I let them make mine for me!"

Arren was silent, pondering this. Presently the mage said, speaking softly, "Do you see, Arren, how an act is not, as young men think, like a rock that one picks up and throws, and it hits or misses, and that's the end of it. When that rock is lifted the earth is lighter, the hand that bears it heavier. When it is thrown the circuits of the stars respond, and where it strikes or falls the universe is changed. On every act the

74

balance of the whole depends. The winds and seas, the powers of water and earth and light, all that these do, and all that the beasts and green things do, is well done, and rightly done. All these act within the Equilibrium. From the hurricane and the great whale's sounding to the fall of a dry leaf and the gnat's flight, all they do is done within the balance of the whole. But we, insofar as we have power over the world and over one another, we must *learn* to do what the leaf and the whale and the wind do of their own nature. We must learn to keep the balance. Having intelligence, we must not act in ignorance. Having choice, we must not act without responsibility. Who am I—though I have the power to do it—to punish and reward, playing with men's destinies?"

"But then," the boy said, frowning at the stars, "is the balance to be kept by doing nothing? Surely a man must act, even not knowing all the consequences of his act, if anything is to be done at all?"

"Never fear. It is much easier for men to act than to refrain from acting. We will continue to do good, and to do evil. . . . But if there were a king over us all again, and he sought counsel of a mage, as in the days of old, and I were that mage, I would say to him: My lord, do nothing because it is righteous, or praiseworthy, or noble, to do so; do nothing because it seems good to do so; do only that which you must do, and which you cannot do in any other way."

There was that in his voice which made Arren turn to watch him as he spoke. He thought that the radiance of light was shining again from his face, seeing the hawk nose and the scarred cheek, the dark, fierce eyes. And Arren looked at him with love but also with fear, thinking, "He is too far above me." Yet as he gazed he became aware at last that it was no magelight, no cold glory of wizardry, that lay shadowless on every line and plane of the man's face, but light itself: morning, the common light of day. There was a power greater than his own. And the years had been no kinder to Sparrowhawk than to any man. Those were lines of age; and he looked tired, as the light grew ever stronger. He yawned. . . .

So gazing, and wondering, and pondering, Arren fell asleep at last. But Sparrowhawk sat by him watching the dawn come and the sun rise, even as one might study a treasure for something gone amiss in it, a jewel flawed, a child sick.

5   Sea Dreams

Late in the morning Sparrowhawk took the magewind from the sail and let his boat go by the world's wind, which blew softly to the south and west. Far off to the right the hills of southern Wathort slipped away and fell behind, growing blue and small, like misty waves above the waves.

Arren woke. The sea basked in the hot, gold noon, endless water under endless light. In the stern of the boat Sparrowhawk sat naked except for a loincloth and a kind of turban made from sailcloth. He was singing softly, striking his palms on the thwart as if it were a drum, in a light monotonous rhythm. The song he sang was no spell of wizardry, no chant or Deed of heroes or kings, but a lilting drone of nonsense words, such as a boy might sing as he herded goats through the long, long afternoons of summer, in the high hills of Gont, alone.

From the sea's surface a fish leaped up and glided through the air for many yards on stiff, shimmering vanes like the wings of dragonflies.

"We're in the South Reach," Sparrowhawk said when his song was done. "A strange part of the world, where the fish fly, and the dolphins sing, they say. But the water's mild for swimming, and I have an understanding with the sharks. Wash the touch of the slave-taker from you."

Arren was sore in every muscle, and loath to move at first. Also he was an unpractised swimmer, for the seas of Enlad are bitter, so that one must fight with them rather than swim in them, and is soon exhausted. This bluer sea was cold at first plunge, then delightful. Aches dropped away from him. He thrashed by *Lookfar*'s side like a young sea-serpent. Spray flew up in fountains. Sparrowhawk joined him, swimming with a firmer stroke. Docile and protective, *Lookfar* waited for them, white-winged on the shining water. A fish leapt from sea to air; Arren pursued it; it dived, leapt up again, swimming in air, flying in the sea, pursuing him.

Golden and supple, the boy played and basked in the water and the light until the sun touched the sea. And dark and spare, with the economy of gesture and the terse strength of age, the man swam, and kept the boat on course, and rigged up an awning of sailcloth, and watched the swimming boy and the flying fish with an impartial tenderness.

"Where are we heading?" Arren asked in the late dusk, after eating largely of salt meat and hardbread, and already sleepy again.

"Lorbanery," Sparrowhawk replied, and the soft meaningless syllables were the last word Arren heard that night, so that his dreams of the early night wove themselves about it. He dreamed he was walking in drifts of soft, pale-coloured stuff, shreds and threads of pink and gold and azure, and felt a foolish pleasure; someone told him, "These are the silkfields of Lorbanery, where it never gets dark." But later, in the fag-end of night, when the stars of autumn shone in the sky of spring, he dreamed that he was in a ruined house. It was dry there. Everything was dusty, and festooned with ragged, dusty webs. Arren's legs were tangled in the webs, and they drifted across his mouth and nostrils, stopping his breath. And the worst horror of it was that he knew the high, ruined room was that hall where he had breakfasted with the Masters, in the Great House on Roke.

He woke all in dismay, his heart pounding, his legs cramped against a thwart. He sat up, trying to get away from the evil dream. In the east there was not yet light, but a dilution of darkness. The mast creaked; the sail, still taut to the north-east breeze, glimmered high and faint above him. In the stern his companion slept sound and silent. Arren lay down again, and dozed till clear day woke him.

This day the sea was bluer and quieter than he had ever imagined it could be, the water so mild and clear that swimming in it was half like gliding or floating upon air; strange it was, and dreamlike.

In the noontime he asked, "Do wizards make much account of dreams?"

Sparrowhawk was fishing. He watched his line attentively. After a long time he said, "Why?"

"I wondered if there's ever truth in them."

"Surely."

"Do they foretell truly?"

But the mage had a bite, and ten minutes later when he had landed their lunch, a splendid silver-blue sea bass, the question was clean forgotten.

In the afternoon as they lazed under the awning rigged to give shelter from the imperious sun, Arren asked, "What do we seek in Lorbanery?"

"That which we seek," said Sparrowhawk.

"In Enlad," said Arren after a while, "we have a story about the boy whose schoolmaster was a stone."

"Aye? . . . What did he learn?"

"Not to ask questions."

Sparrowhawk snorted, as if suppressing a laugh, and sat up. "Very well!" he said. "Though I prefer to save talking till I know what I'm talking about. Why is there no more magic done in Hort Town, and in Narveduen, and maybe throughout all the Reaches? That's what we seek to learn, is it not?"

"Yes."

"Do you know the old saying, *Rules change in the Reaches*? Seamen use it, but it is a wizards' saying, and it means that wizardry itself depends on place. A true spell on Roke may be mere words on Iffish. The language of the Making is not everywhere remembered; here one word, there another. And the weaving of spells is itself interwoven with the earth and the water, the winds, the fall of light, of the place where it is cast. I once sailed far into the East, so far that neither wind nor water heeded my command, being ignorant of their true names; or more likely it was I that was ignorant. For the world is very large, the Open Sea going on past all knowledge; and there are worlds beyond the world. Over these abysses of space and in the long extent of time, I doubt whether any word that can be spoken would bear, everywhere and forever, its weight of meaning and its power; unless it were that First Word which Segoy spoke, making all, or the Final Word which has not been nor will be spoken until all things are unmade. . . . So, even within this world of our Earthsea, the little islands that we know, there are differences, and mysteries, and changes. And the place least known and fullest of mysteries is the South Reach. Few wizards of the Inner Lands have come among these people. They do not welcome wizards, having—so it is believed—their own kinds of magic. But the rumours of these are vague, and it may be that the art magic was never well known here, not fully understood. If so, it would be easily undone by one who set himself to the undoing of it, and sooner weakened than our wizardry of the Inner Lands. And then we might hear tales of the failure of magic in the South. For discipline is the channel in which our acts run strong and deep; where there is no direction, the deeds of men run shallow, and wander, and are wasted. So that fat woman of the mirrors has lost her art, and thinks she never had it. And so Hare takes his hazia and thinks he has gone farther than the greatest mages go, when he has barely entered the fields of dream and is already lost. . . . But where is it that he *thinks* he goes? What is it he looks for? What is it that has swallowed up his wizardry? We have had enough of Hort Town, I think, so we go farther south, to Lorbanery, to see what the wizards do there, to find out what it is that we must find out. . . . Does that answer you?"

"Yes, but—"

"Then let the stone be still a while!" said the mage. And he sat by the mast in the yellowish glowing shade of the awning, and looked out to sea, to the west, as the boat sailed softly southward through the afternoon. He sat erect, and still. The hours passed. Arren swam a couple of times, slipping quietly into the water from the stern of the boat, for he did not like to cross the line of that dark gaze which, looking west over the sea, seemed to see far beyond the bright horizon-line, beyond the blue of air, beyond the boundaries of light.

Sparrowhawk came back from his silence at last, and spoke, though not more than a word at a time. Arren's upbringing had made him quick to sense mood disguised by courtesy or by reserve; he knew his companion's heart was heavy. He asked no more questions, and in the evening he said, "If I sing will it disturb your thoughts?" Sparrowhawk replied with an effort at joking, "That depends upon the singing."

Arren sat with his back against the mast, and sang. His voice was no longer high and sweet as when the music master of the Hall of Berila had trained it years ago, striking the harmonies on his tall harp; nowadays the higher tones of it were husky, and the deep tones had the resonance of a viol, dark and clear. He sang the Lament for the White Enchanter, that song which Elfarran made when she knew of Morred's death and waited for her own. Not often is that song sung, nor lightly. Sparrowhawk listened to the young voice, strong, sure, and sad between the red sky and the sea, and the tears came into his eyes, blinding.

Arren was silent for a while after that song; then he began to sing lesser, lighter tunes, softly, beguiling the great monotony of windless air and heaving sea and failing light, as night came on.

When he ceased to sing everything was still, the wind down, the waves small, wood and rope barely creaking. The sea lay hushed, and over it the stars came out one by one. Piercing bright to the south a yellow light appeared and sent a shower and splintering of gold across the water.

"Look! a beacon!" Then after a minute, "Can it be a star?"

Sparrowhawk gazed at it a while, and finally said," I think it must be the star Gobardon. It can be seen only in the South Reach. Gobardon means Crown. Kurremkarmerruk taught us that, sailing still farther south, one would bring one by one eight more stars clear of the horizon under Gobardon, making a great constellation, some say of a running man, others say of the rune Agnen. The rune of Ending."

They watched it clear the restless sea-horizon and shine forth steadily.

"You sang Elfarran's song," Sparrowhawk said, "as if you knew her grief, and made me know it too. . . . Of all the histories of Earthsea that one has always held me most. The great courage of Morred against despair; and Serriadh who was born beyond despair, the gentle king. And her, Elfarran. When I did the greatest evil I have ever done, yet it was to her beauty that I thought I turned; and I saw her—for a moment I saw Elfarran."

A cold thrill went up Arren's back. He swallowed and sat silent, looking at the splendid, baleful, topaz-yellow star.

"Which of the heroes is yours?" the mage asked, and he answered, "Erreth-Akbe."

"He was indeed the greatest."

"But it is his death I think of: alone, fighting the dragon Orm on the shore of Selidor. He might have ruled all Earthsea. Yet he chose that instead."

The mage did not answer. Each followed his own thoughts a while. Then Arren asked, still watching yellow Gobardon, "Then it is true that the dead can be brought back to life by magery?"

"They can be brought back into life," the mage said.

"But is it ever done? How is it done?"

His companion seemed to answer with very great reluctance. "By the spells of Summoning," he said, and scowled, or winced, as he spoke. Arren thought he would say no more, but presently he went on. "Such spells are in the Lore of Paln. The Master Summoner will not teach or use that Lore. It has been used very seldom; and never wisely, I think. The great spells of it were made by the Grey Mage of Paln, a thousand years ago. He summoned up the spirits of the heroes and mages, even Erreth-Akbe, to give counsel to the Lords of Paln in their wars and government."

"And what happened?"

"The counsel of the dead is not profitable to the living. Paln came on evil times. The Grey Mage was driven forth. He died nameless."

The mage spoke reluctantly, but he did speak, as if he felt Arren had a right to be answered; and Arren pressed on— "Then no one uses those spells now?"

"I have known only one man who used them freely."

"Who was he?"

"He lived in Havnor. They accounted him a mere sorcerer, but in native power he was a great mage. He made money from his art, showing any who paid him whatever spirit they asked to see, dead wife or husband or child, filling his house with unquiet shadows of old centuries, the fair women of the days of the Kings. I saw him summon from the Dry Land my own old master who was Archmage in my youth, Nemmerle, for a trick to entertain the idle. And the great soul came at his call, like a dog to heel. I was angry, and challenged him. I was not Archmage then. I said, 'You compel the dead to come into your house. Will you come with me to theirs?' And I made him come, though he fought me with all his will, and changed his shape, and wept aloud in the darkness."

"So you killed him?" Arren whispered, enthralled.

"No! I made him follow me, and come back with me. He was afraid. He who summoned up the dead so easily was more afraid of death—of his own death—than any man I ever knew. At the wall of stones. . . . But I tell you more than a novice ought to know. And you're not even a novice." Through the dusk the keen eyes returned Arren's gaze, abashing him. "No matter," said the Archmage. "There is a wall of stones, then, at a certain place on the bourne. Across it the spirit goes at death, and a living man may cross it and return again, if he knows the way. . . . By the wall of stones this man crouched down, on the side of the living. He clung to the stones with his hands, and wept and moaned. I made him go on. His fear made me sick and angry. I should have known by that that I did wrong. I was possessed by anger and by vanity. He was strong, and I was eager to prove that I was stronger."

"What did he do afterwards—when you came back?"

"Grovelled, and swore never to use the Pelnish Lore again, and kissed my hand, and would have killed me if he dared."

"What became of him?"

"He went west from Havnor, to Paln perhaps; I heard no more of him. He was white-haired when I knew him, though still a quick, long-armed man, like a wrestler. He would be dead by now. I cannot even bring to mind his name."

"His true name?"

"No! that I can remember—" Then he paused, and for the space of three heartbeats was utterly still.

"They called him Cob, in Havnor," he said in a changed, careful voice. It had grown too dark for expression to be seen. Arren saw him turn and look at the yellow star, now higher above the waves and casting across them a broken trail of gold as slender as a spider's thread. After a time he said, "It's not only in dreams, Arren, that we find ourselves facing what is yet to be in what was long forgotten, and speaking what seems nonsense because we will not see its meaning."

6 Lorbanery

Seen across ten miles of sunlit water, Lorbanery was green, green as the bright moss by a fountain's rim. Close to, it broke up into leaves, and tree-trunks, and shadows, and roads, and houses, and the faces and clothing of people, and dust, and all that goes to make up an island inhabited by men. Yet still, over all, it was green: for every acre of it that was not built or walked upon was given up to the low, round-topped hurbah trees, on the leaves of which feed the little worms that spin the silk that is made into thread and woven by the men, and women, and children of Lorbanery. At dusk the air there is full of small grey bats who feed on the little worms. They eat many, but are suffered to do so, and not killed by the silk-weavers; who indeed account it a deed of very evil omen to kill the grey-winged bats. For if human beings live off the worms, they say, surely small bats have the right to do so.

The houses were curious, with little windows set randomly, and thatches of hurbah-twigs, all green with moss and lichens. It had been a wealthy isle, as isles of the Reach go, and this was still to be seen in the well-painted and well-furnished houses, in the great spinning wheels and looms in the cottages and work-sheds, and in the stone piers of the little harbour of Sosara, where several trading galleys might have docked. But there were no galleys in the harbour. The paint on the houses was faded, and there was no new furniture, and most of the wheels and looms were still, with dust on them, and spiderwebs between pedal and pedal, between warp and frame.

"Sorcerers?" said the mayor of Sosara village, a short man with a face as hard and brown as the soles of his bare feet. "There's no sorcerers in Lorbanery. Nor ever was."

"Who'd have thought it?" said Sparrowhawk admiringly. He was sitting with eight or nine of the villagers, drinking hurbahberry wine, a thin and bitter vintage. He had of necessity told them that he was in the South Reach hunting emmel-stone, but he had in no way disguised himself or his companion, except that Arren had left his sword hidden in the boat, as usual, and if Sparrowhawk had his staff about him it was not to be seen. The villagers had been sullen and hostile at first, and were disposed to turn sullen and hostile again at any moment; only Sparrowhawk's adroitness and authority had forced a grudging acceptance from them. "Wonderful men with trees you must have here," he said now. "What do they do about a late frost on the orchards?"

"Nothing," said a skinny man at the end of the row of villagers. They all sat in a line with their backs against the inn wall, under the eaves of the thatch. Just past their bare feet the large, soft rain of April pattered on the earth.

"Rain's the peril, not frost," the mayor said. "Rots the worm-cases. No man's going to stop rain falling. Nor ever did." He was belligerent against sorcerers and sorcery; some of the others seemed more wistful on the subject. "Never did used to rain this time of year," one of them said, "when the old fellow was alive."

"Who? Old Mildi? Well, he's not alive. He's dead," said the Mayor.

"Used to call him the Orcharder," the skinny man said. "Aye. Called him the Orcharder," said another one. Silence descended, like the rain.

Inside the window of the one-roomed inn Arren sat. He had found an old lute hung on the wall, a long-necked, three-stringed lute such as they play in the Isle of Silk, and he was playing with it now, learning to draw its music from it, not much louder than the patter of the rain on the thatch.

"In the markets in Hort Town," said Sparrowhawk, "I saw stuff sold as silk of Lorbanery. Some of it was silk. But none of it was silk of Lorbanery."

"The seasons have been poor," said the skinny man. "Four years, five years now."

"Five years it is since Fallows Eve," said an old man in a munching, self-satisfied voice, "since old Mildi died, aye, die he did, and not near the age I am. Died on Fallows Eve he did."

"Scarcity puts up the prices," said the mayor. "For one bolt of semi-fine blue-dyed we get now what we used to get for three bolts."

"If we get it. Where's the ships? And the blue's false," said the skinny man, thus bringing on a half-hour argument concerning the quality of the dyes they used in the great worksheds.

"Who makes the dyes?" Sparrowhawk asked, and a new hassle broke out. The upshot of it was that the whole process of dyeing had been overseen by a family who, in fact, called themselves wizards; but if they ever had been wizards they had lost their art, and nobody else had found it, as the skinny man remarked sourly. For they all agreed, except the mayor, that the famous blue dyes of Lorbanery and the unmatchable crimson, the 'dragon's fire' worn by Queens in Havnor long ago, were not what they had been. Something had gone out of them. The unseasonable rains were at fault, or the dye-earths, or the refiners. "Or the eyes," said the skinny man, "of men who couldn't tell the true azure from blue mud," and he glared at the mayor. The mayor did not take up the challenge; they fell silent again.

The thin wine seemed only to acidify their tempers, and their faces looked glum. There was no sound now but the rustle of rain on the uncountable leaves of the orchards of the valley, and the whisper of the sea down at the end of the street, and the murmur of the lute in the darkness within doors.

"Can he sing, that girlish lad of yours?" asked the mayor.

"Aye, he can sing. Arren! sing a measure for us, lad."

"I cannot get this lute to play out of the minor," said Arren at the window, smiling. "It wants to weep. What would you hear, my hosts?"

"Something new," growled the mayor.

The lute thrilled a little; he had the touch of it already. "This might be new here," he said. Then he sang.

> By the white straits of Soléa
> and the bowed red branches
> that bent their blossoms over
> her bowed head, heavy
> with sorrow for the lost lover,
> by the red branch and the white branch
> and the sorrow unceasing
> do I swear, Serriadh,
> son of my mother and of Morred,
> to remember the wrong done
>   forever, forever.

They were still: the bitter faces and the shrewd, the hard-worked hands and bodies. They sat still in the warm rainy Southern dusk, and heard that song like the cry of the grey swan of the cold seas of Éa, yearning, bereft. For a while after the song was over they kept still.

"That's a queer music," said one, uncertainly.

Another, reassured as to the absolute centrality of the isle of Lorbanery in all time and space, said, "Foreign music's always queer and gloomy."

"Give us some of yours," said Sparrowhawk. "I'd like to hear a cheery stave myself. The lad will always sing of old dead heroes."

"I'll do that," said the last speaker, and hemmed a bit, and started out to sing about a lusty, trusty, barrel of wine, and a hey, ho, and about we go! But nobody joined him in the chorus, and he went flat on the hey, ho.

"There's no more proper singing," he said angrily. "It's the young people's fault, always chopping and changing the way things are done, and not learning the old songs."

"It's not that," said the skinny man, "there's no more proper anything. Nothing goes right any more."

"Aye, aye, aye," wheezed the oldest one, "the luck's run out. That's what. The luck's run out."

After that there was not much to say. The villagers departed by twos and threes, until Sparrowhawk was left alone outside the window, and Arren inside it. And then Sparrowhawk laughed, at last. But it was not a merry laugh.

The innkeeper's shy wife came and spread out beds for them on the floor, and went away, and they lay down to sleep. But the high rafters of the room were an abode of bats. In and out the unglazed window the bats flew all night long, chittering very high. Only at dawn did they all return and settle, each composing itself in a little, neat, grey package hanging from a rafter upside down.

Perhaps it was the restlessness of the bats that made Arren's sleep uneasy. It was many nights now since he had slept ashore; his body was not used to the immobility of earth, and insisted to him as he fell asleep that he was rocking, rocking . . . and then the world would fall out from underneath him and he would wake with a great start. When at last he got to sleep he dreamed he was chained in the hold of the slaver's ship; there were others with him, but they were all dead. He woke from this dream more than once, struggling to get free of it, but falling to sleep at once re-entered it. At last it seemed to him that he was all alone on the ship, but still chained so that he could not move. Then a curious, slow voice spoke in his ear. "Loose your bonds," it said. "Loose your bonds." He tried to move then, and moved: he stood up. He was on some vast, dim moor, under a heavy sky. There was horror in the earth, in the thick air, an enormity of horror. This place was fear, was fear itself, and he in it, and no paths. He must find the way, but there were no paths, and he was tiny, like a child, like an ant, and the place was huge, endless. He tried to walk, stumbled, woke.

The fear was inside him, now that he was awake, and he was not inside it: yet it was no less huge and endless. He felt choked by the black darkness of the room, and looked for stars in the dim square that was the window, but though the rain had ceased there were no stars. He lay awake, and was afraid, and the bats flew in and out on noiseless leather wings. Sometimes he heard their thin voices at the very limit of his hearing.

The morning came bright, and they were early up. Sparrowhawk inquired earnestly for emmel-stone. Though none of the townsfolk knew what emmel-stone was, they all had theories about it, and quarrelled over them; and he listened, though he listened for news of something other than emmel-stone. At last he and Arren took a way that the mayor suggested to them, towards the quarries where the blue dye-earth was dug. But on the way Sparrowhawk turned aside.

"This will be the house," he said. "They said that that family of dyers and discredited magicians lives on this road."

"Is it any use to talk to them?" said Arren, remembering Hare all too well.

"There is a centre to this bad luck," said the mage, harshly. "There is a place where the luck runs out. I need a guide to that place!" And he went on, and Arren must follow.

The house stood apart among its own orchards, a fine building of stone, but it and all its acreage had gone long uncared for. Cocoons of ungathered silkworms hung discoloured among the ragged branches, and the ground beneath was thick with a papery litter of dead grubs and moths. All about the house under the close-set trees there hung an odour of decay, and as they came to it Arren suddenly remembered the horror that had been on him in the night.

Before they reached the door it was flung open. Out charged a grey-haired woman, glaring with reddened eyes and shouting, "Out, curse you, thieves slanderers lackwits liars and misbegotten fools! Get out, out, go! The ill chance be on you forever!"

Sparrowhawk stopped, looking somewhat amazed, and quickly raised his hand in a curious gesture. He said one word, "Avert!"

At that the woman stopped yelling. She stared at him.

"Why did you do that?"

"To turn your curse aside."

She stared a while longer and said at last, hoarsely, "Foreigners?"

"From the North."

She came forward. At first Arren had been inclined to laugh at her, an old woman screeching on her doorstep, but close to her he felt only shame. She was foul and ill-clothed, and her breath stank, and her eyes had a terrible stare of pain.

"I have no power to curse," she said. "No power." She imitated Sparrowhawk's gesture. "They still do that, where you come from?"

He nodded. He watched her steadily, and she returned his gaze. Presently her face began to work and change, and she said, "Where's thy stick?"

"I do not show it here, sister."

"No, you should not. It will keep you from life. Like my power, it kept me from life. So I lost it. I lost all the things I knew, all the words and names. They came by little strings like spiderwebs out of my eyes and mouth. There is a hole in the world, and the light is running out of it. And the words go with the light. Did you know that? My son sits staring all day at the

92

dark, looking for the hole in the world. He says he would see better if he were blind. He has lost his hand as a dyer. We were the Dyers of Lorbanery. Look!" She shook before them her muscular, thin arms, stained to the shoulder with a faint, streaky mixture of ineradicable dyes. "It never comes off the skin," she said, "but the mind washes clean. It won't hold the colours. Who are you?"

Sparrowhawk said nothing. Again his eyes held the woman's; and Arren, standing aside, watched uneasily.

All at once she trembled and said in a whisper, "I know thee—"

"Aye. Like knows like, sister."

It was strange to see how she pulled away from the mage in terror, wanting to flee him, and yearned towards him as if to kneel at his feet.

He took her hand and held her. "Would you have your power back, the skills, the names? I can give you that."

"You are the Great Man," she whispered. "You are the King of the Shadows, the Lord of the Dark Place—"

"I am not. I am no king. I am a man, a mortal, your brother and your like."

"But you will not die?"

"I will."

"But you will come back, and live for ever."

"Not I. Nor any man."

"Then you are not—not the Great One in the darkness," she said, frowning, and looking at him a little askance, with less fear. "But you are a Great One. Are there two? What is your name?"

Sparrowhawk's stern face softened a moment. "I cannot tell you that," he said gently.

"I'll tell you a secret," she said. She stood straighter now, facing him, and there was the echo of an old dignity in her voice and bearing. "I do not want to live, and live, and live forever. I would rather have back the names of things. But they are all gone. Names don't matter now. There are no more secrets. Do you want to know my name?" Her eyes filled with light, her fists clenched, she leaned forward and whispered: "My name is Akaren." Then she screamed aloud, "Akaren! Akaren! My name is Akaren! Now they all know my secret name, my true name, and there are no secrets, and there is no truth, and there is no death—death—death!" She screamed the word sobbing, and spittle flew from her lips.

"Be still, Akaren!"

She was still. Tears ran down her face, which was dirty, and streaked with locks of her uncombed grey hair.

Sparrowhawk took that wrinkled, tear-blubbered face between his hands and very lightly, very tenderly, kissed her on the eyes. She stood motionless, her eyes closed. Then with his lips close to her ear he spoke a little in the Old Speech, and once more kissed her, and let her go.

She opened clear eyes, and looked at him a while with a brooding, wondering gaze. So a newborn child looks at its mother; so a mother looks at her child. She turned slowly and went to her door, and entered it, and closed it behind her: all in silence, with the still look of wonder on her face.

In silence the mage turned and started back towards the road. Arren followed him. He dared ask no question. Presently the mage stopped, there in the ruined orchard, and said, "I took her name from her, and gave her a new one. And thus in some sense a re-birth. There was no other help or hope for her."

His voice was strained and stifled.

"She was a woman of power," he went on. "No mere witch or potion-maker, but a woman of art and skill, using her craft for the making of the beautiful, a proud woman, and honourable. That was her life. And it is all wasted." He turned abruptly away, walked off into the orchard aisles, and there stood beside a tree-trunk, his back turned.

Arren waited for him in the hot, leaf-speckled sunlight. He

knew that Sparrowhawk was ashamed to burden Arren with his emotion; and indeed there was nothing the boy could do or say. But his heart went out utterly to his companion, not now with that first romantic ardour and adoration, but painfully, as if a link were drawn forth from the very inmost of it and forged into an unbreaking bond. For in this love he now felt there was compassion: without which love is untempered, and is not whole, and does not last.

Presently Sparrowhawk returned to him through the green shade of the orchard. Neither said anything, and they went on side by side. It was hot already; last night's rain had dried and dust rose under their feet on the road. Earlier the day had seemed dreary and insipid to Arren, as if infected by his dreams; now he took pleasure in the bite of the sunlight and the relief of shade, and enjoyed walking without brooding about their destination.

This was just as well, for they accomplished nothing. The afternoon was spent in talking with the men who mined the dye-ores, and bargaining for some bits of what was said to be emmel-stone. As they trudged back to Sosara with the late sun pounding on their heads and necks, Sparrowhawk remarked, "It's blue malachite; but I doubt they'll know the difference in Sosara either."

"They're strange here," Arren said. "It's that way with everything, they don't know the difference. Like what one of them said to the headman last night, 'You wouldn't know the true azure from blue mud. . . .' They complain about bad times, but they don't know when the bad times began; they say the work's shoddy, but they don't improve it; they don't even know the difference between an artisan and a spell-worker, between handcraft and the art magic. It's as if they had no lines and distinctions and colours clear in their heads. Everything's the same to them, everything's grey."

"Aye," said the mage, thoughtfully. He stalked along for a

while, his head hunched between his shoulders, hawklike; though a short man he walked with a long stride. "What is it they're missing?"

Arren said without hesitation, "Joy in life."

"Aye," said Sparrowhawk again, accepting Arren's statement and pondering it for some time. "I'm glad," he said at last, "that you can think for me, lad. . . . I feel tired and stupid. I've been sick at heart since this morning, since we talked to her who was Akaren. I do not like waste, and destruction. I do not want an enemy. If I must have an enemy I do not want to seek him, and find him, and meet him. . . . If one must hunt, the prize should be a treasure, not a detestable thing."

"An enemy, my lord," said Arren.

Sparrowhawk nodded.

"When she talked about the Great Man, the King of Shadows—?"

Sparrowhawk nodded again. "I think so," he said. "I think we must come not only to a place, but to a person. This is evil, evil, what passes on this island, this loss of craft and pride, this joylessness, this waste. This is the work of an evil will. But a will not even bent here, not even noticing Akaren, or Lorbanery. The track we hunt is a track of wreckage, as if we followed a runaway cart down a mountainside, and watched it set off an avalanche."

"Could she—Akaren—tell you more about this enemy—who he is and where he is, or *what* he is?"

"Not now, lad," the mage said in a soft but rather bleak voice. "No doubt she could have. In her madness there was still wizardry. Indeed her madness was her wizardry. But I could not hold her to answer me. She was in too much pain."

And he walked on with his head somewhat hunched between his shoulders, as if himself enduring, and longing to avoid, some pain.

Arren turned, hearing a scuffling of feet behind them on the road. A man was running after them, a good way off but catching up fast. The dust of the road and his long wiry hair made aureoles of red about him in the westering light, and his long shadow hopped fantastically along the trunks and aisles of the orchards by the road. "Listen!" he shouted. "Stop! I found it! I found it!"

He caught up with them in a rush. Arren's hand went first to the air where his swordhilt might have been, then to the air where his lost knife had been, and then made itself into a fist, all in half a second. He scowled and moved forward. The man was a full head taller than Sparrowhawk, and broad-shouldered, and a panting, raving, wild-eyed madman. "I found it!" he kept saying while Arren, trying to dominate him by a stern threatening voice and attitude, said, "What do you want?" The man tried to get around him, to Sparrowhawk; Arren stepped in front of him again.

"You are the Dyer of Lorbanery," Sparrowhawk said.

Then Arren felt he had been a fool, trying to protect his companion; and he stepped aside, out of the way. For at six words from the mage, the madman stopped his panting and the clutching gesture of his big, stained hands; his eyes grew quieter; he nodded his head.

"I was the dyer," he said, "but now I can't dye." Then he looked askance at Sparrowhawk, and grinned; he shook his head with its reddish, dusty bush of hair. "You took away my mother's name," he said. "Now I don't know her, and she doesn't know me. She loves me well enough still, but she's left me. She's dead."

Arren's heart contracted, but he saw that Sparrowhawk merely shook his head a little. "No, no," he said, "she's not dead."

"But she will be. She'll die."

"Aye. That's a consequence of being alive," the mage said. The Dyer seemed to puzzle this over for a minute, and then came right up to Sparrowhawk, seized his shoulders, and bent over him. He moved so fast that Arren could not prevent him, but he did come up very close, and so heard his whisper, "I found the hole in the darkness. The King was standing there. He watches it, he rules it. He had a little flame, a little candle in his hand. He blew on it, and it went out. Then he blew on it again and it burned! It burned!"

Sparrowhawk made no protest at being held and whispered at. He simply asked, "Where were you when you saw that?"

"In bed."

"Dreaming?"

"No."

"Across the wall?"

"No," the Dyer said, in a suddenly sober tone, and as if uncomfortable. He let the mage go, and took a step back from him. "No, I—I don't know where it is. I found it. But I don't know where."

"That's what I'd like to know," said Sparrowhawk.

"I can help you."

"How?"

"You have a boat. You came here on it, you're going on. Are you going on west? That's the way. The way to the place where he comes out. There has to be a place, a place *here*, because he's alive—not just the spirits, the ghosts, that come over the wall, not like that,—you can't bring anything but souls over the wall but this is the body, this is the flesh immortal. I saw the flame rise in the darkness at his breath, the flame that was out. I saw that." The man's face was transfigured, a wild beauty in it in the long red-gold light. "I know that he has overcome death. I know it. I gave my wizardry to know it. I was a wizard once! And you know it, and you are going there. Take me with you."

The same light shone on Sparrowhawk's face, but left it unmoved and harsh. "I am trying to go there," he said.

"Let me go with you!"

Sparrowhawk nodded briefly. "If you're there when we sail," he said, as coldly as before.

The Dyer backed away from him another step, and stood watching him, the exaltation in his face clouding slowly over until it was replaced by a strange, heavy look; it was as if reasoning thought were labouring to break through the storm of words and feelings and visions that confused him. Finally he turned around without a word and began to run back down the road, into the haze of dust that had not yet settled on his tracks. Arren drew a long breath of relief.

Sparrowhawk also sighed, though not as if his heart were any easier. "Well," he said. "Strange roads have strange guides. Let's go on."

Arren fell into step beside him. "You won't take him with us?" he asked.

"That's up to him."

With a flash of anger Arren thought: It's up to me, also. But he did not say anything, and they went on together in silence.

They were not well received on their return to Sosara. Everything on a little island like Lorbanery is known as soon as it is done, and no doubt they had been seen turning aside to the Dyers' House, and talking to the madman on the road. The innkeeper served them uncivilly, and his wife acted scared to death of them. In the evening when the men of the village came to sit under the eaves of the inn, they made much display of not speaking to the foreigners, and being very witty and merry among themselves. But they had not much wit to pass around, and soon ran short of jollity. They all sat in silence for a long time, and at last the mayor said to Sparrowhawk, "Did you find your blue rocks?"

"I found some blue rocks," Sparrowhawk replied politely.

"Sopli showed you where to find 'em, no doubt."

Ha, ha, ha, went the other men, at this masterstroke of irony.

"Sopli would be the red-haired man?"

"The madman. You called on his mother in the morning."

"I was looking for a wizard," said the wizard.

The skinny man, who sat nearest him, spat into the darkness. "What for?"

"I thought I might find out about what I'm looking for."

"People come to Lorbanery for silk," the mayor said. "They don't come for stones. They don't come for charms. Or arm-wavings and jibber-jabber and sorcerers' tricks. Honest folk live here and do honest work."

"That's right. He's right," said others.

"And we don't want any other sort here, people from foreign parts snooping about and prying into our business."

"That's right. He's right," came the chorus.

"If there was any sorcerer around that wasn't crazy we'd give him an honest job in the sheds, but they don't know how to do honest work."

"They might, if there were any to do," said Sparrowhawk. "Your sheds are empty, the orchards are untended, the silk in your warehouses was all woven years ago. What do you do, here in Lorbanery?"

"We look after our own business," the mayor snapped, but the skinny man broke in excitedly, "Why don't the ships come, tell us that! What are they doing in Hort Town? Is it because our work's been shoddy?—" He was interrupted by angry denials. They shouted at one another, jumped to their feet, the mayor shook his fist in Sparrowhawk's face, another drew a knife. Their mood had gone wild. Arren was on his feet at once, and looked at Sparrowhawk expecting to see him stand up in the sudden radiance of the magelight and strike them dumb with his revealed power. But he did not. He sat there, and looked from one to another, and listened to their menaces. And gradually they fell quiet, as if they could not keep up anger any more than they could keep up merriment. The knife was sheathed, the threats turned to sneers. They began to go off like dogs leaving a dog-fight, some strutting and some sneaking.

When the two were left alone Sparrowhawk got up, and came inside the inn, and took a long draught of water from the jug beside the door. "Come, lad," he said. "I've had enough of this."

"To the boat?"

"Aye." He put down two trade-counters of silver on the window sill to pay for their lodging, and hoisted up their light pack of clothing. Arren was tired and sleepy, but he looked around the room of the inn, stuffy and bleak, and all aflitter up in the rafters with the restless bats; he thought of last night in that room, and followed Sparrowhawk willingly. He thought, too, as they went down Sosara's one, dark street, that going now they would give the madman Sopli the slip. But when they came to the harbour he was waiting for them on the pier.

"There you are," said the mage. "Get aboard, if you want to come."

Without a word Sopli got down into the boat and crouched beside the mast, like a big unkempt dog. At this Arren rebelled. "My lord!" he said. Sparrowhawk turned; they stood face to face on the pier above the boat.

"They are all mad on this island, but I thought you were not. Why do you take him?"

"As a guide."

"A guide—to more madness? To death by drowning or a knife in the back?"

"To death, but by what road I do not know."

Arren spoke with heat, and though Sparrowhawk answered quietly there was something of a fierce note in his voice. He was not used to being questioned. But ever since Arren had tried to protect him from the madman on the road that afternoon, and had seen how vain and unneeded his protection was, he had felt a bitterness, and all that uprush of devotion he had felt in the morning was spoilt and wasted. He was unable to protect

Sparrowhawk; he was not permitted to make any decisions; he was unable, or was not permitted, even to understand the nature of their quest. He was merely dragged along on it, useless as a child. But he was not a child.

"I would not quarrel with you, my lord," he said as coldly as he could. "But this—this is beyond reason!"

"It is beyond all reason. We go where reason will not take us. Will you come, or will you not?"

Tears of anger sprang into Arren's eyes. "I said I would come with you and serve you. I do not break my word."

"That is well," the mage said grimly, and made as if to turn away. Then he faced Arren again. "I need you, Arren; and you need me. For I will tell you now that I believe this way we go is yours to follow, not out of obedience or loyalty to me, but because it was yours to follow before you ever saw me; before you ever set foot on Roke; before you sailed from Enlad. You cannot turn back from it."

His voice had not softened. Arren answered him as grimly, "How should I turn back, with no boat, here on the edge of the world?"

"This is the edge of the world? No, that is farther on. We may yet come to it."

Arren nodded once, and swung down into the boat. Sparrowhawk loosed the line and spoke a light wind into the sail. Once away from the looming, empty docks of Lorbanery the air blew cool and clean out of the dark north, and the moon broke silver from the sleek sea before them, and rode upon their left as they turned southward to coast the isle.

7 The Madman

The madman, the Dyer of Lorbanery, sat huddled up against the mast, his arms wrapped around his knees and his head hunched down. His mass of wiry hair looked black in the moonlight. Sparrowhawk had rolled himself up in a blanket and gone to sleep in the stern of the boat. Neither of them stirred. Arren sat up in the prow; he had sworn to himself to watch all night. If the mage chose to assume that their lunatic passenger would not assault him, or Arren, in the night, that was all very well for him; Arren, however, would make his own assumptions, and undertake his own responsibilities.

But the night was very long, and very calm. The moonlight poured down, changeless. Huddled by the mast, Sopli snored, long, soft snores. Softly the boat moved onward; softly Arren slid into sleep. He started awake once, and saw the moon scarcely higher; he abandoned his self-righteous guardianship, made himself comfortable, and went to sleep.

He dreamed again, as he seemed always to do on this voyage, and at first the dreams were fragmentary but strangely sweet and reassuring. In place of *Lookfar*'s mast a tree grew, with great arching arms of foliage; swans guided the boat, swooping on strong wings before it; far ahead, over the beryl-green sea, shone a city of white towers. Then he was in one of those towers, climbing the steps which spiralled upward, running up them lightly and eagerly. These scenes changed and recurred and led into others, which passed without trace; but suddenly he was in the dreaded dull twilight on the moors, and the horror grew in him until he could not breathe. But he went forward, because he must go forward. After a long time he realised that to go forward here was to go in a circle and come round on one's own tracks again. Yet he must get out, get away, it grew more and more urgent. He began to run. As he ran the circles narrowed in and the ground began to slant. He was running in the darkening gloom, faster and faster, around the sinking inner lip of a pit, an enormous whirlpool sucking down to darkness; and as he knew this, his foot slipped, and he fell.

"What's the matter, Arren?"

Sparrowhawk spoke to him from the stern. Grey dawn held the sky and sea still.

"Nothing."

"The nightmare?"

"Nothing."

Arren was cold, and his right arm ached from having been cramped under him. He shut his eyes against the growing light and thought, "He hints of this and hints of that, but he will never tell me clearly where we're going, or why, or why I should go there. And now he drags this madman with us. Which is maddest, the lunatic or I, for coming with him? The two of them may understand each other, it's the wizards who are mad now, he said. I could have been at home by now, at home in the Hall in Berila, in my room with the carven walls, and the red rugs on the floor, and a fire in the hearth, waking up to go out a-hawking with my father. Why did I come with him? Why did he bring me? Because it's my way to go, he says, but that's wizard's talk, making things seem great by great words. But the meaning of the words is always somewhere else. If I have any way to go, it's to my home, not wandering senselessly across the Reaches. I have duties at home, and am shirking them. If he really thinks there is some enemy of wizardry at work, why did he come alone, with me? He might have brought another mage to help him—a hundred of them. He could have brought an army of warriors, a fleet of ships. Is this how a great peril is met, by sending out an old man and a boy in a boat? This is mere folly. He is mad himself; it is as he said, he seeks death. He seeks death, and wants to take me with him. But I am not mad and not old, I will not die, I will not go with him."

He sat up on his elbow, looking forward. The moon that had risen before them as they left Sosara Bay was again before them, sinking. Behind, in the east, day came wan and dull. There were no clouds, but a faint sickly overcast. Later in the day the sun grew hot, but it shone veiled, without splendour.

All day long they coasted Lorbanery, low and green to their right hand. A light wind blew off the land and filled their sail. Towards evening they passed a long last cape; the breeze died down. Sparrowhawk spoke the magewind into the sail, and like a falcon loosed from the wrist *Lookfar* started and fled forward eagerly, putting the Isle of Silk behind.

Sopli the Dyer had cowered in the same place all day, evidently afraid of the boat and afraid of the sea, seasick and wretched. He spoke now, hoarsely. "Are we going west?"

The sunset was right in his face; but Sparrowhawk, patient with his stupidest questions, nodded.

"To Obehol?"

"Obehol lies west of Lorbanery."

"A long way west. Maybe the place is there."

"What is it like, the place?"

"How do I know? How could I see it? It's not on Lorbanery! I hunted for it for years, four years, five years, in the dark, at night, shutting my eyes, always with him calling *Come, come,* but I couldn't come. I'm no lord of wizards who can tell the ways in the dark. But there's a place to come to in the light, under the sun, too. That's what Mildi and my mother wouldn't understand. They kept looking in the dark. Then old Mildi died, and my mother lost her mind. She forgot the spells we use in the dyeing, and it affected her mind. She wanted to die, but I told her to wait. Wait till I find the place. There must be a place. If the dead can come back to life in the world there must be a place in the world where it happens."

"Are the dead coming back to life?"

"I thought you knew such things," Sopli said after a pause, looking askance at Sparrowhawk.

"I seek to know them."

Sopli said nothing. The mage suddenly looked at him, a direct compelling gaze, though his tone was gentle: "Are you looking for a way to live forever, Sopli?"

Sopli returned his gaze for a moment; then he hid his shaggy, brownish-red head in his arms, locking his hands across his ankles, and rocked himself a little back and forth. It seemed that when he was frightened he took this position, and when he was in it he would not speak or take any notice of what was said. Arren turned away from him in despair and disgust. How could they go on, with Sopli, for days or weeks, in an eighteen-foot boat? It was like sharing a body with a diseased soul. . . .

Sparrowhawk came up beside him in the prow, and knelt with one knee on the thwart, looking into the sallow evening. He said, "The man has a gentle spirit."

Arren did not answer this. He asked coldly, "What is Obehol? I never heard the name."

"I know its name and place on the charts; no more. . . . Look there: the companions of Gobardon!"

The great topaz-coloured star was higher in the south now, and beneath it, just clearing the dim sea, shone a white star to the left and a bluish-white one to the right, forming a triangle.

"Have they names?"

"The Master Namer did not know. Maybe the men of

Obehol and Wellogy have names for them. I do not know. We go now into strange seas, Arren, under the Sign of Ending."

The boy did not answer, looking with a kind of loathing at the bright, nameless stars above the endless water.

As they sailed westward day after day the warmth of the southern spring lay on the waters, and the sky was clear. Yet it seemed to Arren that there was a dullness in the light, as if it fell aslant through glass. The sea was lukewarm when he swam, bringing little refreshment. Their salt food had no savour. There was no freshness or brightness in any thing, unless it were at night, when the stars burned with a greater radiance than he had ever seen in them. He would lie and watch them till he slept. Sleeping, he would dream: always the dream of the moors, or the pit, or a valley hemmed round by cliffs, or a long road going downwards under a low sky; always the dim light, and the horror in him, and the hopeless effort to escape.

He never spoke of this to Sparrowhawk. He did not speak of anything important to him, nothing but the small daily incidents of their sailing; and Sparrowhawk, who had always had to be drawn out, was now habitually silent.

Arren saw now what a fool he had been to entrust himself body and soul to this restless and secretive man, who let impulse move him and made no effort to control his life, nor even to save it. For now the fey mood was on him; and that, Arren thought, was because he dared not face his own failure—the failure of wizardry as a great power among men.

It was clear now that to those who knew the secrets, there were not many secrets to that art magic from which Sparrowhawk, and all the generations of sorcerers and wizards, had made much fame and power. There was not much more to it than the use of wind and weather, the knowledge of healing herbs, and a skilful show of such illusions as mists and lights and shape-changes, which could awe the ignorant, but which were mere tricks. Reality was not changed. There was nothing in magery that gave a man true power over men; nor was it any use against death. The mages lived no longer than ordinary men. All their secret words could not put off for one hour the coming of their death.

Even in small matters magery was not worth counting on. Sparrowhawk was always miserly about employing his arts; they went by the world's wind whenever they might, they fished for food, and spared their water, like any sailors. After four days of interminable tacking into a fitful headwind, Arren asked him if he would not speak a little following wind into the sail, and when he shook his head, said, "Why not?"

"I would not ask a sick man to run a race," said Sparrowhawk, "nor lay a stone on an overburdened back." It was not clear whether he spoke of himself, or of the world at large. Always his answers were grudging, hard to understand. There, thought Arren, lay the very heart of wizardry: to hint at mighty meanings while saying nothing at all, and to make doing nothing at all seem the very crown of wisdom.

Arren had tried to ignore Sopli, but it was impossible; and in any case he soon found himself in a kind of alliance with the madman. Sopli was not so mad, or not so simply mad, as his wild hair and fragmented talk made him appear. Indeed the maddest thing about him was perhaps his terror of the water. To come into a boat had taken desperate courage, and he never really got the edge worn off his fear; he kept his head down so much so that he would not have to see the water heaving and lapping about him, and the frail little shell of the boat. To stand up in the boat made him giddy; he clung to the mast. The first time Arren decided on a swim and dived off the prow, Sopli shouted out in horror; when Arren came climbing back into the boat, the poor man was green with shock. "I thought you were drowning yourself," he said, and Arren had to laugh.

In the afternoon, when Sparrowhawk sat meditating, unheeding and unhearing, Sopli came hitching cautiously over the thwarts to Arren. He said in a low voice, "You don't want to die, do you?"

"Of course not."

"He does," Sopli said, with a little shift of his lower jaw towards Sparrowhawk.

"Why do you say that?"

Arren took a lordly tone, which indeed came naturally to him, and Sopli accepted it as natural, though he was ten or fifteen years older than Arren. He replied with ready civility, though in his usual fragmentary way, "He wants to get to the secret place. But I don't know why. He doesn't want. . . . He doesn't believe in . . . the promise."

"What promise?"

Sopli glanced up at him sharply, something of his ruined manhood in his eyes; but Arren's will was stronger. He answered very low, "You know. Life. Eternal life."

A great chill went through Arren's body. He remembered his dreams, the moor, the pit, the cliffs, the dim light. That was death, that was the horror of death. It was from death he must escape, must find the way. And on the doorsill stood the figure crowned with shadow, holding out a little light no larger than a pearl, the glimmer of immortal life.—Arren met Sopli's eyes for the first time: light brown eyes, very clear; in them he saw that he had understood at last, and that Sopli shared his knowledge.

"He," the Dyer said, with his twitch of the jaw towards Sparrowhawk, "he won't give up his name. Nobody can take his name through. The way is too narrow."

"Have you seen it?"

"In the dark, in my mind. That's not enough. I want to get there, I want to see it. In the world, with my eyes. What if I— what if I died and couldn't find the way, the place? Most people can't find it, they don't even know it's there, there's only some of us have the power. But it's hard, because you have to give the power up to get there. . . . No more words. No more names. It is too hard to do in the mind. And when you—die, your mind—dies." He stuck each time on the word. "I want to *know* I can come back. I want to be there. On the side of life. I want to live, to be safe. I hate—I hate this water. . . ."

The Dyer drew his limbs together as a spider does when falling, and hunched his wiry-red head down between his shoulders, to shut out the sight of the sea.

But Arren did not shun his conversation after that, knowing that Sopli shared not only his vision, but his fear; and that, if worst came to worst, Sopli might aid him against Sparrowhawk.

Always they sailed, slowly in the calms and fitful breezes, to the west, where Sparrowhawk pretended that Sopli guided them. But Sophi did not guide them, he who knew nothing of the sea, had never seen a chart, never been in a boat, dreaded the water with a sick dread. It was the mage who guided them, and led them deliberately astray. Arren saw this now, and saw the reason of it. The Archmage knew that they, and others like them, were seeking eternal life, and had been promised it or drawn towards it, and might find it. In his pride, his overween-ing pride as Archmage, he feared lest they might gain it; he envied them, and feared them, and would have no man greater than himself. He meant to sail out onto the Open Sea beyond all lands until they were utterly astray and could never come back to the world, and there they would die of thirst. For he would die himself, to prevent them from eternal life.

Every now and then there would come a moment, when Sparrowhawk spoke to Arren of some small matter of managing the boat or swam with him in the warm sea or bade him good night under the great stars, when all these ideas seemed utter nonsense to the boy. He would look at his companion and see him, that hard, harsh, patient face, and he would think, "This is my lord and friend." And it seemed unbelievable to him that he had doubted. But a little while later he would be doubting again, and he and Sopli would exchange glances, warning each other of their mutual enemy.

Every day the sun shone hot, yet dull. Its light lay like a gloss on the slow-heaving sea. The water was blue, the sky blue without change or shading. The breezes blew and died, and they turned the sail to catch them, and slowly crept on towards no end.

One afternoon they had at last a light following wind; and Sparrowhawk pointed upward, near sunset, saying, "Look." High above the mast a line of sea-geese wavered like a black rune drawn across the sky. The geese flew westward: and following, on the next day *Lookfar* came in sight of a great island.

"That's it," Sopli said. "That land. We must go there."

"The place you seek is there?"

"Yes. We must land there. This is as far as we can go."

"This land will be Obehol. Beyond it in the South Reach is another island, Wellogy. And in the West Reach are islands lying farther west than Wellogy. Are you certain, Sopli?"

The Dyer of Lorbanery grew angry, so that the wincing look came back into his eyes; but he did not talk madly, Arren thought, as he had when they first spoke with him many days ago on Lorbanery. "Yes. We must land here. We have gone far enough. The place we seek is here. Do you want me to swear that I know it? Shall I swear by my name?"

"You cannot," Sparrowhawk said, his voice hard, looking up at Sopli who was taller than he; Sopli had stood up, holding on tight to the mast, to look at the land ahead. "Don't try, Sopli."

The Dyer scowled as if in rage or pain. He looked at the mountains lying blue with distance before the boat, over the heaving, trembling plain of water, and said, "You took me as guide. This is the place. We must land here."

"We'll land in any case, we must have water," said Sparrow-hawk, and went to the tiller. Sopli sat down in his place by the mast, muttering. Arren heard him say, "I swear by my name. By my name," many times, and each time he said it, he scowled again as if in pain.

They beat closer to the island on a northwind, and coasted it seeking a bay or landing, but the breakers beat thunderous in the hot sunlight on all the northern shore. Inland green mountains stood baking in that light, tree-clothed to the peaks.

Rounding a cape they came at last in sight of a deep crescent bay with white sand beaches. Here the waves came in quietly, their force held off by the cape, and a boat might land. No sign of human life was visible on the beach or in the forests above it; they had not seen a boat, a roof, a wisp of smoke. The light breeze dropped as soon as *Lookfar* entered the bay. It was still, silent, hot. Arren took the oars, Sparrowhawk steered. The creak of the oars in the locks was the only sound. The green peaks loomed above the bay, closing in around. The sun laid sheets of white-hot light on the water. Arren heard the blood drumming in his ears. Sopli had left the safety of the mast and crouched in the prow, holding onto the gunwales, staring and straining forward to the land. Sparrowhawk's dark, scarred face shone with sweat as if it had been oiled; his glance shifted continually from the low breakers to the foliage-screened bluffs above.

"Now," he said to Arren and the boat. Arren struck three great strokes with the oars, and lightly *Lookfar* came up on the sand. Sparrowhawk leapt out to push the boat clear up on the last impetus of the waves. As he put his hands out to push he stumbled and half fell, catching himself against the stern. With a mighty strain he dragged the boat back into the water on the outward wash of the wave, and floundered in over the gunwale as she hung between sea and shore. "Row!" he gasped out, and crouched on all fours, streaming with water and trying to get his breath. He was holding a spear—a bronze-headed throwing spear two feet long. Where had he got it? Another spear appeared as Arren hung bewildered on the oars; it struck a thwart edgewise, splintering the wood, and rebounded end over end. On the low bluffs over the beach, under the trees, figures moved, darting and crouching. There were little whistling, whirring noises in the air. Arren suddenly bent his head between his shoulders, bent his back, and rowed with powerful strokes: two to clear the shallows, three to turn the boat, and away.

Sopli, in the prow of the boat, behind Arren's back, began to shout. Arren's arms were seized suddenly so that the oars shot up out of the water, and the butt of one struck him in the pit of the stomach, so that for a moment he was blind and breathless. "Turn back! Turn back!" Sopli was shouting. The boat leapt in the water all at once, and rocked. Arren turned as soon as he had got his grip on the oars again, furious. Sopli was not in the boat.

All around them the deep water of the bay heaved and dazzled in the sunlight.

Stupidly, Arren looked behind him again, then at Sparrowhawk crouching in the stern. "There," Sparrowhawk said, pointing alongside, but there was nothing, only the sea and the dazzle of the sun. A spear from a throwing-stick fell short of the boat by a few yards, entered the water noiselessly, vanished. Arren rowed ten or twelve hard strokes, then backed water, and looked once more at Sparrowhawk.

Sparrowhawk's hands and left arm were bloody; he held a wad of sailcloth to his shoulder. The bronze-headed spear lay in the bottom of the boat. He had not been holding it when Arren first saw it; it had been standing out from the hollow of his shoulder where the point had gone in. He was scanning the water between them and the white beach, where some tiny figures hopped and wavered in the heat-glare. At last he said, "Go on."

"Sopli—"

"He never came up."

"Is he drowned?" Arren asked unbelieving.

Sparrowhawk nodded.

Arren rowed on until the beach was only a white line beneath the forests and the great green peaks. Sparrowhawk sat by the tiller, holding the wad of cloth to his shoulder but paying no heed to it.

"Did a spear hit him?"

"He jumped."

"But he—he couldn't swim. He was afraid of the water!"

"Aye. Mortally afraid. He wanted. . . . He wanted to come to land."

"Why did they attack us? Who are they?"

"They must have thought us enemies. Will you . . . give me a hand with this a moment?" Arren saw then that the cloth he held pressed against his shoulder was soaked and vivid.

The spear had struck between the shoulder-joint and collarbone, tearing one of the great veins, so that it bled heavily. Under his direction Arren tore strips from a linen shirt and made shift to bandage the wound. Sparrowhawk asked him for the spear, and when Arren laid it on his knees he put his right hand over the blade, long and narrow like a willow leaf, of crudely hammered bronze; he made as if to speak, but after a minute he shook his head. "I have no strength for spells," he said. "Later. It will be all right. Can you get us out of this bay, Arren?"

Silently the boy returned to the oars. He bent his back to the work, and soon, for there was strength in his smooth, lithe frame, he brought *Lookfar* out of the crescent bay into open water. The long noon calm of the Reach lay on the sea. The sail hung slack. The sun glared through a veil of haze, and the green peaks seemed to shake and throb in the great heat. Sparrowhawk had stretched out in the bottom of the boat, his head propped against the thwart by the tiller; he lay still, lips and eyelids half-parted. Arren did not like to look at his face, but stared over the boat's stern. Heat-haze wavered above the water, as if veils of cobweb were spun out over the sky. His arms trembled with fatigue, but he rowed on.

"Where are you taking us?" Sparrowhawk asked hoarsely, sitting up a little. Turning, Arren saw the crescent bay curving its green arms about the boat once more, and the white line of the beach ahead, and the mountains gathered in the air above. He had turned the boat around without knowing it.

"I can't row any more," he said, and stowed the oars, and went and crouched in the prow. He kept thinking Sopli was behind him in the boat, by the mast. They had been many days together, and his death had been too sudden, too reasonless to be understood. Nothing was to be understood.

The boat hung swaying on the water, the sail slack on the spar. The tide, beginning to enter the bay, turned her slowly broadside to the current and pushed her by little nudges in and in, towards the distant white line of the beach.

"*Lookfar*," the mage said caressingly, and a word or two in the Old Speech; and softly the boat rocked and nosed outward and slipped over the blazing sea away from the arms of the bay.

But as slowly and softly, in less than an hour, she ceased to make way, and again the sail hung slack. Arren looked back in the boat and saw his companion lying as before, but his head had dropped back a little, and his eyes were closed.

All this while Arren had felt a heavy, sickly horror, which grew on him and held him from action as if winding his body in fine threads, and dimming his mind. No courage rose up in him to fight against the fear, only a kind of dull resentment against his lot.

He should not let the boat drift here near the rocky shores of a land whose people attacked strangers; this was clear to his mind, but it did not mean much. What was he to do instead?

Row the boat back to Roke? He was lost, utterly lost beyond
hope, in the vastness of the Reach. He could never bring the
boat back through those weeks of voyage to any friendly land.
Only with the mage's guidance could he do it, and Sparrowhawk was hurt and helpless, as suddenly and meaninglessly
as Sopli was dead. His face was changed, lax-featured and
yellowish; he might be dying. Arren thought that he should go
and move him under the awning to keep the sunlight off him,
and give him water; men who had lost blood needed to drink.
But they had been short of water for days; the barrel was
almost empty. What did it matter? There was no good in
anything, no use. The luck had run out.

Hours went by, the sun beat down, the greyish heat wrapped
Arren round. He sat unmoving.

A breath of cool passed across his forehead. He looked up.
It was evening: the sun was down, the west dull red. *Lookfar*
moved slowly under a mild breeze from the east, skirting the
steep, wooded shores of Obehol.

Arren went back in the boat and looked after his companion,
arranging him a pallet under the awning, and giving him water
to drink. He did these things hurriedly, and kept his eyes from
the bandage, which was in need of changing, for the wound
had not wholly ceased to bleed. Sparrowhawk, in the languor
of weakness, did not speak; even as he drank eagerly, his eyes
closed and he slipped into sleep again, that being the greater
thirst. He lay silent; and when in the darkness the breeze died,
no magewind replaced it, and again the boat rocked idly on the
smooth, heaving water. But now the mountains that loomed
to the right were black against a sky gorgeous with stars, and
for a long time Arren gazed at them. Their outlines seemed
familiar to him, as if he had seen them before, as if he had
known them all his life.

When he lay down to sleep he faced southward, and there,
well up in the sky above the blank sea, burned the star

Gobardon. Beneath it were the two forming a triangle with it, and beneath these three had risen in a straight line, forming a greater triangle. Then, slipping free of the liquid plains of black and silver, two more followed as the night wore on; they were yellow like Gobardon, though fainter, slanting from right to left from the right base of the triangle. So there were eight of the nine stars which were supposed to make the figure of a man, or the Hardic rune Agnen. To Arren's eyes there was no man in the pattern, unless, as star-figures are, he was strangely distorted; but the rune was plain, with hooked arm and cross-stroke, all but the foot, the last stroke to complete it, the star that had not yet risen.

Watching for it, Arren slept.

When he woke in the dawn, *Lookfar* had drifted farther from Obehol. A mist hid the shores and all but the peaks of the mountains, and thinned out into a haze above the violet waters of the south, dimming the last stars.

He looked at his companion. Sparrowhawk breathed unevenly, as when pain moves under the surface of sleep not quite breaking it. His face was lined and old in the cold shadowless light. Arren looking at him saw a man with no power left in him, no wizardry, no strength, not even youth, nothing. He had not saved Sopli, nor turned away the spear from himself. He had brought them into peril, and had not saved them. Now Sopli was dead, and he dying, and Arren would die. Through this man's fault; and in vain, for nothing.

So Arren looked at him with the clear eyes of despair, and saw nothing.

No memory stirred in him of the fountain under the rowan tree, or of the white magelight on the slave-ship in the fog, or of the weary orchards of the House of the Dyers. Nor did any pride or stubbornness of will wake in him. He watched dawn come over the quiet sea, where low, great swells ran coloured like pale amethyst, and it was all like a dream, pallid, with no grip or vigour of reality. And at the depths of the dream and of the sea, there was nothing—a gap, a void. There were no depths.

The boat moved forward irregularly and slowly, following the fitful humour of the wind. Behind, the peaks of Obehol shrank black against the rising sun, from which the wind came, bearing the boat away from land, away from the world, out onto the open sea.

8   The Children of the Open Sea

Towards the middle of that day Sparrowhawk stirred, and asked
for water. When he had drunk he asked, "Where are we heading?" For the sail was taut above him, and the boat dipped
like a swallow on the long swells.

"West, or north by west."

"I'm cold," Sparrowhawk said. The sun blazed down, filling
the boat with heat.

Arren said nothing.

"Try to hold west. Wellogy, west of Obehol. Land there.
We need water."

The boy looked forward, over the empty sea.

"What's the matter, Arren?"

He said nothing.

Sparrowhawk tried to sit up, and failing that, to reach his
staff that lay by the gear-box; but it was out of his reach,
and when he tried to speak again the words halted on his dry
lips. The blood broke out anew under the soaked and crusted
bandage, making a little spider's thread of crimson on the
dark skin of his chest. He drew breath sharply and closed his
eyes.

Arren looked at him, but without feeling, and not for long.
He went forward and resumed his crouching position in the

prow, gazing forward. His mouth was very dry. The east wind that now blew steady over the open sea was as dry as a desert wind. There were only two or three pints of water left in their cask; these were, in Arren's mind, for Sparrowhawk, not for himself; it never occurred to him to drink from that water. He had set out fishing lines, having learned since they left Lorbanery that raw fish fulfils both thirst and hunger; but there was never anything on the lines. It did not matter. The boat moved on over the desert of water. Over the boat, slowly, yet winning the race in the end by all the width of heaven, the sun moved also from east to west.

Once Arren thought he saw a blue height in the south that might have been land, or cloud; the boat had been running somewhat north of west for hours. He did not try to tack and turn, but let her go on. The land might or might not be real; it did not matter. To him all the vast fiery glory of wind and light and ocean was dim and false.

Darkness came, and light again, and dark, and light, like drumbeats on the tight-stretched canvas of the sky.

He trailed his hand in the water over the side of the boat. For an instant he saw that, vivid: his hand pale greenish beneath the living water. He bent and sucked the wet off his fingers. It was bitter, burning his lips painfully, but he did it again. Then he was sick, and crouched down vomiting, but only a little bile burned his throat. There was no more water to give Sparrowhawk, and he was afraid to go near him. He lay down, shivering despite the heat. It was all silent, dry, and bright: terribly bright. He hid his eyes from the light.

They stood in the boat, three of them, stalk-thin and angular, great-eyed, like strange, dark herons or cranes. Their voices were thin, like birds' voices. He did not understand them. One knelt above him with a dark bladder on his arm, and tipped from it into Arren's mouth: it was water. Arren drank avidly, choked, drank again till he had drained the container. Then he looked about, and struggled to his feet, saying, "Where is, where is he?" For in *Lookfar* with him were only the three strange, slender men.

They looked at him uncomprehending.

"The other man," he croaked, his raw throat and stiff-caked lips unfit to form the words, "my friend—"

One of them understood his distress if not his words, and putting a slight hand on his arm, pointed with the other. "There," he said, reassuring.

Arren looked. And he saw, ahead of the boat and northward of her, some gathered in close and others strung far out across the sea, rafts: so many rafts that they lay like autumn leaves on a pool. Low to the water, each bore one or two cabins or huts near the centre, and several had masts stepped. Like leaves they floated, rising and falling very softly as the vast swells of the western ocean passed under them. The lanes of water shone like silver between them, and over them towered great violet and golden rainclouds, darkening the west.

"There," the man said, pointing to a great raft near *Lookfar*. "Alive?"

They all looked at him, and at last one understood. "Alive. He is alive." At this Arren began to weep, a dry sobbing, and one of the men took his wrist in a strong and narrow hand and drew him out of *Lookfar* and onto a raft to which the boat had been made fast. The raft was so great and buoyant that it did not dip even slightly to their weight. The man led Arren across it, while one of the others reached out with a heavy gaff tipped with a curving whaleshark's tooth and hauled a nearby raft closer, till they could step the gap. There he led Arren to the shelter or cabin, which was open on one side and closed with woven screens on the fourth. "Lie down," he said, and beyond that Arren knew nothing at all.

He was lying on his back, stretched out flat, gazing up at a rough green roof dappled with tiny dots of light. He thought he was in the apple orchards of Semermine, where the princes of Enlad pass their summers, in the hills behind Berila; he thought he was lying in the thick grass at Semermine, looking up at the sunlight between apple boughs.

After a while he heard the slap and jostle of water in the hollow places underneath the raft, and the thin voices of the raft-people speaking a tongue that was the common Hardic of the Archipelago, but much changed in sounds and rhythms, so that it was hard to understand; and so he knew where he was—out beyond the Archipelago, beyond the Reach, beyond all isles, lost on the open sea. But still he was untroubled, lying as comfortably as if he lay in the grass in the orchards of his home.

He thought after a while that he ought to get up, and did so, finding his body very thin and burnt-looking, and his legs shaky but serviceable. He pushed aside the woven hanging that made the walls of the shelter and stepped out into the afternoon. It had rained while he slept. The wood of the raft, great, smooth-shapen, squared logs, fit close and caulked, was dark with wet, and the hair of the thin, half-naked people was black and lank from the rain. But half the sky was clear where the sun stood in the west, and the clouds now rode to the far north-east in heaps of silver.

One of the men came up to Arren, warily, stopping some feet from him. He was slight and short, no taller than a boy of twelve; his eyes were long, large, and dark. He carried a spear with a barbed ivory head.

Arren said to him, "I owe my life to you and your people."

The man nodded.

"Will you take me to my companion?"

Turning away, the raft-man raised his voice in a high, piercing cry like the call of a seabird. Then he squatted down on his heels as if to wait, and Arren did the same.

The rafts had masts, though the mast of the one they were on was not stepped. On these, sails could be run up, small compared to the breadth of the raft, of a brown material, not canvas or linen but a fibrous stuff that looked not woven but beaten together, as felt is made. A raft some quarter mile away let the brown sail down from the crosstree by ropes and slowly worked its way, gaffing and poling off the other rafts between, till it came alongside the one Arren was on. When there was only three feet of water between, the man beside Arren got up and nonchalantly hopped across. Arren did the same and landed awkwardly on all fours; there was no spring left in his knees. He picked himself up, and found the little man looking at him, not with amusement, but with approval: Arren's composure had evidently won his respect.

This raft was larger and higher out of the water than any other, made of logs forty feet in length and four or five feet wide, blackened and smooth with use and weather. Strangely carven statues of wood stood about the several shelters or enclosures on it, and tall poles bearing tufts of seabirds' feathers stood at the four corners. His guide took him to the smallest of the shelters, and there he saw Sparrowhawk lying asleep.

Arren sat down inside the shelter. His guide went back to the other raft, and nobody bothered him. After an hour or so a woman from the other raft brought him food: a kind of cold fish-stew with bits of some transparent green stuff in it, salty but good; and a small cup of water, stale, tasting pitchy from the caulking of the barrel. He saw by the way she gave him the water that it was a treasure that she gave him, a thing to be honoured. He drank it respectfully and asked for no more, though he could have drunk ten times the cupful.

Sparrowhawk's shoulder had been skilfully bandaged; he slept deep and easily. When he woke up his eyes were clear. He looked at Arren, and smiled the sweet, joyous smile that was always startling on his hard face. Arren felt suddenly like weeping again. He put his hand on Sparrowhawk's hand and said nothing.

One of the raft-folk approached, and squatted down in the shade of the large shelter nearby: a kind of temple, it appeared to be, with a square design of great complexity above the door-way, and the doorjambs made of logs carved in the shape of grey whales sounding. This man was short and thin like the others, boy-like in frame, but his face was strong-featured and weathered by the years. He wore nothing but a loincloth, but dignity clothed him amply. "He must sleep," he said, and Arren left Sparrowhawk and came to him.

"You are the chief of this folk," Arren said, knowing a prince when he saw one.

"I am," the man said, with a short nod. Arren stood before him, erect and unmoving. Presently the man's dark eyes met his briefly: "You are a chief also," he observed.

"I am," Arren answered. He would have liked very much to know how the raft-man knew it, but remained impassive. "But I serve my lord, there."

The chief of the raft-folk said something Arren did not understand at all: certain words changed out of recognition, or names he did not know; then he said, "Why came you into Balatran?"

"Seeking—"

But Arren did not know how much to say, nor indeed what to say. All that had happened, and the matter of their quest, seemed very long ago, and was confused in his mind. At last he said, "We came to Obehol. They attacked us when we came to land. My lord was hurt."

"And you?"

"I was not hurt," Arren said, and the cold self-possession he had learnt in his courtly childhood served him well. "But there was—there was something like a madness. One who was with us drowned himself. There was a fear—" He stopped, and stood silent.

The chief watched him with black, opaque eyes. At last he said, "You come by chance here, then."

"Yes. Are we still in the South Reach?"

"Reach? No. The islands—" The chief moved his slender, black hand in an arc, no more than a quarter of the compass, north to east. "The islands are there," he said. "All the islands." Then showing all the evening sea before them, from north through west to south, he said, "The sea."

"What land are you from, lord?"

"No land. We are the Children of the Open Sea."

Arren looked at his keen face. He looked about him at the great raft with its temple and its tall idols, each carved from a single tree, great god-figures mixed of dolphin, fish, man, and seabird; at the people busy at their work, weaving, carving, fishing, cooking on raised platforms, tending babies; at the other rafts, seventy at least, scattered out over the water in a great circle perhaps a mile across. It was a town: smoke rising in thin wisps from distant houses, the voices of children high on the wind. It was a town, and under its floors was the abyss.

"Do you never come to land?" the boy asked in a low voice.

"Once each year. We go to the Long Dune. We cut wood there and refit the rafts. That is in autumn, and after that we follow the grey whales north. In winter we go apart, each raft alone. In the spring we come to Balatran, and meet. There is going from raft to raft then, there are marriages, the Long Dance is held. These are the Roads of Balatran; from here the great current bears south. In summer we drift south upon the great current, until we see the Great Ones, the grey whales, turning northward. Then we follow them, returning at last to the beaches of Emah on the Long Dune, for a little while."

"This is most wonderful, my lord," said Arren. "Never did I hear of such a people as yours. My home is very far from here.

Yet there too, in the island of Enlad, we dance the Long Dance on midsummer eve."

"You stamp the earth down, and make it safe," the chief said dryly. "We dance on the deep sea."

After a time he asked, "How is he called, your lord?"

"Sparrowhawk," Arren said. The chief repeated the syllables, but they clearly had no meaning for him. And that more than any other thing made Arren understand that his tale was true, that these people lived on the sea year in, year out, on the open sea past any land or scent of land, beyond the flight of the land birds, outside the knowledge of men.

"There was death in him," the chief said. "He must sleep. You go back to Star's raft; I will send for you." He stood up. Though perfectly sure of himself, he was apparently not quite sure what Arren was, whether he should treat him as an equal or as a boy. Arren preferred the latter, in this situation, and accepted his dismissal; but then faced a problem of his own. The rafts had drifted apart again, and a hundred yards of satiny water rippled between the two.

The chief of the Children of the Open Sea spoke to him once more, briefly. "Swim," he said.

Arren let himself gingerly into the water. Its cool was pleasant on his sun-baked skin. He swam across and hauled himself out on the other raft, to find a group of five or six children and young people watching him with undisguised interest. A very small girl said, "You swim like a fish on a hook."

"How should I swim?" asked Arren, a little mortified, but polite; indeed he could not have been rude to a human being so very small. She looked like a polished mahogany statuette, fragile, exquisite. "Like this!" she cried, and dived like a seal into the dazzle and liquid roil of the waters. Only after a long time, and at an improbable distance, did he hear her shrill cry and see her black, sleek head above the surface.

"Come on," said a boy who was probably Arren's age, though

he looked not more than twelve in height and build: a grave-faced fellow, with a blue crab tattooed all across his back. He dived, and all dived, even the three-year-old; so Arren had to, and did so, trying not to splash.

"Like an eel," said the boy, coming up by his shoulder.

"Like a dolphin," said a pretty girl with a pretty smile, and vanished in the depths.

"Like me!" squeaked the three-year-old, bobbing like a bottle.

So that evening until dark, and all the next long golden day, and the days that followed, Arren swam and talked and worked with the young people of Star's raft. And of all the events of his voyage since that morning of the equinox when he and Sparrow-hawk left Roke, this seemed to him in some way the strangest; for it had nothing to do with all that had gone before, in the voyage or in all his life; and even less to do with what was yet to come. At night, lying down to sleep among the others under the stars, he thought, "It is as if I were dead, and this is an after-life, here in the sunlight, beyond the edge of the world, among the sons and daughters of the sea. . . ." Before he slept he would look in the far south for the yellow star and the figure of the Rune of Ending, and always he saw Gobardon, and the lesser or the greater triangle; but it rose later now, and he could not keep his eyes open till the whole figure stood free of the horizon. By night and by day the rafts drifted southward, but there was never any change in the sea, for the ever-changing does not change; the rainstorms of May passed over, and at night the stars shone, and all day the sun.

He knew that their life could not be lived always in this dreamlike ease. He asked of winter, and they told him of the long rains and the mighty swells, the single rafts, each separated from all the rest, drifting and plunging along through the grey and darkness, week after week after week. Last winter in a month-long storm they had seen waves so great they were "like thunderclouds", they said, for they had not seen hills: from the back of one the next could be seen, immense, miles away, rushing hugely towards them. Could the rafts ride such seas? he asked, and they said yes, but not always. In the spring when they gathered at the Roads of Balatran there would be two rafts missing, or three, or six. . . .

They married very young. Bluecrab, the boy tattooed with his namesake, and the pretty girl Albatross were man and wife, though he was just seventeen and she two years younger; there were many such marriages between the rafts. Many babies crept and toddled about the rafts, tied by long leashes to the four posts of the central shelter, all crawling into it in the heat of the day and sleeping in wriggling heaps. The older children tended the younger, and men and women shared in all the work. All took their turn at gathering the great brown-leaved seaweeds, the *nilgu* of the Roads, fringed like fern and eighty or a hundred feet long. All worked together at pounding the nilgu into cloth and braiding the coarse fibres for ropes and nets; at fishing, and drying the fish, and shaping whale-ivory into tools, and all the other tasks of the rafts. But there was always time for swimming, and for talking, and never a time by which a task must be finished. There were no hours: only whole days, whole nights. After a few such days and nights it seemed to Arren that he had lived on the raft for time uncountable, and Obehol was a dream, and behind that were fainter dreams, and in some other world he had lived on land and been a prince in Enlad.

When he was summoned at last to the chief's raft, Sparrowhawk looked at him a while and said, "You look like that Arren whom I saw in the Court of the Fountain: sleek as a golden seal. It suits you here, lad."

"Aye, my lord."

"But where is here? We have left places behind us. We have sailed off the maps. . . . Long ago I heard tell of the Raft-Folk, but thought it only one more tale of the South Reach, a fancy without substance. Yet we were rescued by that fancy, and our lives saved by a myth."

He spoke smilingly, as though he had shared in that timeless ease of life in the summer light; but his face was gaunt, and in his eyes lay an unlighted darkness. Arren saw that, and faced it.

"I betrayed—" he said, and stopped. "I betrayed your trust in me."

"How so, Arren?"

"There—at Obehol. When for once you needed me. You were hurt, and needed my help. I did nothing. The boat drifted, and I let her drift. You were in pain and I did nothing for you. I saw land—I saw land, and did not even try to turn the boat—"

"Be still, lad," the mage said with such firmness that Arren obeyed. And presently, "Tell me what you thought at that time."

"Nothing, my lord—nothing! I thought there was no use in doing anything. I thought your wizardry was gone—no, that it had never been. That you had tricked me." The sweat broke out on Arren's face and he had to force his voice, but he went on. "I was afraid of you. I was afraid of death. I was so afraid of it I would not look at you, because you might be dying. I could think of nothing, except that there was—there was a way of not dying, for me, if I could find it. But all the time life was running out, as if there was a great wound and the blood running from it—such as you had. But this was in everything. And I did nothing, nothing, but try to hide from the horror of dying."

He stopped, for saying the truth aloud was unendurable. It was not shame that stopped him, but fear, the same fear. He knew now why this tranquil life in sea and sunlight on the rafts seemed to him like an after-life or a dream, unreal. It was because he knew in his heart that reality was empty: without life, or warmth, or colour, or sound: without meaning. There were no heights or depths. All this lovely play of form and light and colour on the sea and in the eyes of men, was no more than that: a playing of illusions on the shallow void.

They passed, and there remained the shapelessness and the cold. Nothing else.

Sparrowhawk was looking at him, and he had looked down to avoid that gaze. But there spoke in him unexpectedly a little voice of courage, or perhaps of mockery. It was arrogant, and pitiless, and it said, Coward! Coward! Will you throw even this away?

So he looked up, with a great effort of will, and met his companion's eyes.

Sparrowhawk reached out and took his hand in a hard grasp, so that both by eye and by flesh they touched.

"Lebannen," he said. He had never spoken Arren's true name, nor had Arren told it to him. "Lebannen, this is. And thou art. There is no safety. There is no end. The word must be heard in silence. There must be darkness to see the stars. The dance is always danced above the hollow place, above the terrible abyss."

Arren would have drawn away from him, but the mage did not release him. "I failed you," he said. "I will fail you again. I have not strength enough!"

"You have strength enough." Sparrowhawk's voice seemed tender, but in it was that same hardness that had risen in the depths of Arren's own shame, mocking. "What you love, you will love. What you undertake, you will do. You are to be relied on. Small wonder if you have not learned that yet; you have had only seventeen years to learn it. But consider, Lebannen. To refuse death is to refuse life."

"But I sought death!" Arren lifted his head and stared at Sparrowhawk. "Like Sopli—"

"Sopli was not seeking death. He sought an end to the fear of death."

"But there is a way. The way he looked for. Sopli. And Hare,

130

and the others. The way back to life, life without death. You—you above all—you must know of that way—"

"I do not know it."

"But the others, the wizards—"

"I know what they think they seek. But I know that they will die, as Sopli did. That I will die. That you will die."

The hard grip still held Arren.

"And I prize that knowledge. It is a great gift. It is the gift of selfhood. For only that is ours which we are willing to lose. That selfhood, our torment and glory, our humanity, does not endure. It changes and it goes, a wave on the sea. Would you have the sea grow still and the tides cease to save one wave, to save yourself? Would you give up the craft of your hands, and the passion of your heart, and the hunger of your mind, to buy safety?"

"Safety," Arren repeated.

"Aye," the mage said. "Safety."

He released Arren then; let his hand go, and looked away from him, leaving him alone, though they still sat face to face.

"I do not know," Arren said at last. "I do not know what I seek, or where I go, or who I am."

"I know who you are," Sparrowhawk said in that same low, hard voice. "You are my guide. In your innocence and courage, in your unwisdom and your loyalty, you are my guide—the child I send before me into the dark. It is your fear I follow. You have thought me harsh to you. You never knew how harsh. I use your love as a man burns a candle, burns it away, to light his steps. And we must go on. We must go on. We must go all the way. We must come to the place where the springs run dry, the place to which your mortal terror draws you."

"Where is it, my lord?"

"I do not know."

"I cannot lead you there. But I will come with you."

The mage's gaze on him was sombre, unfathomable.

"But if I should fail again, and betray you—"

"I will trust you, son of Morred."

Then both were silent.

Above them the tall carven idols rocked very slightly against the blue Southern sky, dolphin bodies, gulls' wings folded, human faces with staring eyes of shell.

Sparrowhawk got up, stiffly, for he was still far from being fully healed of his wound. "I am tired of sitting about," he said, "I shall grow fat in idleness." He began to pace the length of the raft, and Arren joined him. They talked a little as they walked; Arren told Sparrowhawk how he spent his days, who his friends among the raft-folk were. Sparrowhawk's restlessness was greater than his strength, which soon gave out. He stopped by a girl who was weaving nilgu on her loom behind the House of the Great Ones, asking her to seek out the chief for him, and then returned to his shelter. There the chief of the raft-folk came, and greeted him with courtesy, which the mage returned; and all three of them sat down together on the spotted sealskin rugs of the shelter.

"I have thought," the chief began, slowly and with a civil solemnity, "of the things you have told me. Of how men think to come back from death into their own bodies, and seeking to do this forget the worship of the gods and neglect their bodies and go mad. This is an evil matter and a great folly. Also I have thought, what has it to do with us? We have nothing to do with other men, their islands and their ways, their makings and unmakings. We live on the sea and our lives are the sea's. We do not hope to save them, we do not seek to lose them. Madness does not come here. We do not come to land, nor do the land-folk come to us. When I was young, we spoke sometimes with men who came on boats to the Long Dune, when we were there to cut the raft-logs and build the winter shelters. Often we saw sails from Ohol and Welwai (so he called Obehol and Wellogy) following the grey whales in the autumn. Often they followed our rafts from afar, for we know the roads and meeting-places of the Great Ones in the sea. But that is all I ever saw of the land-folk, and now they come no longer. Maybe they have all gone mad and fought with one another. Two years ago on the long Dune looking north to Welwai we saw for three days the smoke of a great burning. And if that were so, what is it to us? We are the Children of the Open Sea. We go the sea's way."

"Yet seeing a landsman's boat adrift you came to it," said the mage.

"Some among us said it was not wise to do so, and would have let the boat drift on to sea's end," the chief answered in his high, impassive voice.

"You were not one of them."

"No. I said, though they be land-folk, yet we will help them, and so it was done. But with your undertakings we have nothing to do. If there is a madness among the land-folk, the land-folk must deal with it. We follow the road of the Great Ones. We cannot help you in your search. So long as you wish to stay with us you are welcome. It is not many days till the Long Dance; after it we return northward, following the eastern current that by summer's end will bring us round again to the seas by the Long Dune. If you will stay with us and be healed of your hurt, this will be well. Or if you will take your boat and go your way, this too will be well."

The mage thanked him, and the chief got up, slight and stiff as a heron, and left them alone together.

"In innocence there is no strength against evil," said Sparrowhawk, a little wryly. "But there is strength in it for good. . . . We shall stay with them a while, I think, till I am cured of this weakness."

"That is wise," said Arren. Sparrowhawk's physical frailty had shocked and moved him; he had determined to protect the man from his own energy and urgency, to insist that they wait at least until he was free of pain before they went on.

The mage looked at him, somewhat startled by the compliment.

"They are kind, here," Arren pursued, not noticing. "They seem to be free of that sickness of soul they had in Hort Town, and the other islands. Maybe there is no island where we would have been helped and welcomed, as these lost people have done."

"You may well be right."

"And they lead a pleasant life, in summer. . . ."

"They do. Though to eat cold fish one's whole life long, and never to see a pear-tree in blossom, or taste of a running spring, would be wearisome at last!"

So Arren returned to Star's raft, and worked and swam and basked with the other young people, and talked with Sparrowhawk in the cool of the evening, and slept under the stars. And the days wore on towards the Long Dance of midsummer's eve, and the great rafts drifted slowly southward on the currents of the open sea.

9 Orm Embar

All night long, the shortest night of the year, torches burned on the rafts which lay gathered in a great circle under the thick-starred sky, so that a ring of fires flickered on the sea. The raft-folk danced, using no drum or flute or any music but the rhythm of bare feet on the great rocking rafts, and the thin voices of their chanters ringing plaintive in the vastness of their dwelling-place the sea. There was no moon that night, and the bodies of the dancers were dim in the starlight and torch-light. Now and again one flashed like a fish leaping, a youth vaulting from one raft to the next: long leaps, and high, and they vied with one another, trying to circle all the ring of rafts and dance on each, and so come round before the break of day.

Arren danced with them, for the Long Dance is held on every isle of the Archipelago, though the steps and songs may vary. But as the night drew on, and many dancers dropped out and settled down to watch or doze, and the voices of the chanters grew husky, he came with a group of high-leaping lads to the chief's raft, and there stopped, while they went on.

Sparrowhawk sat with the chief and the chief's three wives, near the temple. Between the carven whales that made its door-way sat a chanter whose high voice had not flagged all night long. Tireless he sang, tapping his hands on the wooden deck to keep the time.

"What does he sing of?" Arren asked the mage, for he could not follow the words, which were all held long, with trills and strange catches on the note.

"Of the grey whales, and the albatross, and the storm. . . . They do not know the songs of the heroes and the kings. They do not know the name of Erreth-Akbe. Earlier he sang of Segoy, how he established the lands amid the sea; that much they remember of the lore of men. But the rest is all of the sea."

Arren listened; he heard the singer imitate the whistling cry of the dolphin, weaving his song about it. He watched Sparrow-hawk's profile against the torchlight, black and firm as rock, and saw the liquid gleam of the chief's wives' eyes as they chatted softly, and felt the long slow dip of the raft on the quiet sea, and slipped gradually towards sleep.

He roused all at once: the chanter had fallen silent. Not only the one near whom they sat, but all the others, on the rafts near and far. The thin voices had died away like a far-off piping of seabirds, and it was still.

Arren looked over his shoulder to the east, expecting dawn. But only the old moon rode low, just rising, golden among the summer stars.

Then looking southward he saw, high up, yellow Gobardon, and below it the eight companions, even to the last: the rune of Ending clear and fiery above the sea. And turning to Sparrow-hawk, he saw the dark face turned to those same stars.

"Why do you cease?" the chief was asking the singer. "It is not daybreak, not even dawn."

The man stammered and said, "I do not know."

"Sing on! The Long Dance is not ended."

"I do not know the words," the chanter said, and his voice rose high as if in terror. "I cannot sing. I have forgotten the song."

"Sing another, then!"

"There are no more songs. It is ended," the chanter cried, and bent forward till he crouched on the decking; and the chief stared at him in amazement.

The rafts rocked beneath their sputtering torches, all silent. The silence of the ocean enclosed the small stir of life and light upon it, and swallowed it. No dancer moved.

It seemed to Arren then that the splendour of the stars dimmed, and yet no daylight was in the east. A horror came on him, and he thought, "There will be no sunrise. There will be no day."

The mage stood up. As he did so a faint light, white and quick, ran along his staff, burning clearest in the rune that was set in silver in the wood. "The dance is not ended," he said, "nor the night. Arren, sing."

Arren would have said, "I cannot, lord!"—but instead he looked at the nine stars in the south, and drew a deep breath, and sang. His voice was soft and husky at first, but it grew stronger as he sang, and the song was that oldest song, of the Creation of Éa, and the balancing of the dark and the light, and the making of green lands by him who spoke the first word, the Eldest Lord, Segoy.

Before the song was ended the sky had paled to greyish-blue, and in it only the moon and Gobardon still burned faintly, and the torches hissed in the wind of dawn. Then, the song done, Arren was silent; and the dancers who had gathered to listen returned quietly from raft to raft, as the light brightened in the east.

"That is a good song," the chief said. His voice was uncertain, though he strove to speak impassively. "It would not be well to end the Long Dance before it is completed. I will have the lazy chanters beaten with nilgu thongs."

"Comfort them rather," Sparrowhawk said. He was still afoot, and his tone was stern. "No singer chooses silence. Come with me, Arren."

He turned to go to the shelter, and Arren followed him. But the strangeness of that daybreak was not yet done, for even then, as the eastern rim of the sea grew white, there came from the north flying a great bird: so high up that its wings caught the sunlight that had not shone upon the world yet, and beat in strokes of gold upon the air. Arren cried out, pointing. The mage looked up, startled. Then his face became fierce and exulting, and he shouted out aloud, *"Nam hietha arw Ged arkvaissa!"*—which in the Speech of the Making is, If thou seekest Ged here find him.

And like a golden plummet dropped, with wings held high outstretched, vast and thundering on the air, with talons which might seize an ox as if it were a mouse, with a curl of steamy flame streaming from long nostrils, the dragon stooped like a falcon on the rocking raft.

The raft-folk cried out; some cowered down, some leapt into the sea, and some stood still, watching, in a wonder that surpassed fear.

The dragon hovered above them. Ninety feet, maybe, was he from tip to tip of his vast membranous wings, that shone in the new sunlight like gold-shot smoke, and the length of his body was no less, but lean, arched like a greyhound, clawed like a lizard, and snake-scaled. Along the narrow spine went a row of jagged darts, like rose-thorns in shape, but at the hump of the back three feet in height, and so diminishing that the last at the tail-tip was no longer than the blade of a little knife. These thorns were grey, and the scales of the dragon were iron-grey, but there was a glitter of gold in them. His eyes were green and slitted.

Moved by fear for his people to forget fear for himself, the chief of the raft-folk came from his shelter with a harpoon such as they used in the hunt of whales: it was longer than himself, and pointed with a great barbed point of ivory. Poising it on his small sinewy arm he ran forward to gain the impetus to hurl it up and strike the dragon's narrow, light-mailed belly that hung above the raft. Arren waking from stupor saw him, and plunging forward caught his arm and came down in a heap with him and the harpoon. "Would you anger him with your silly pins?" he gasped. "Let the Dragonlord speak first!"

The chief, half the wind knocked out of him, stared stupidly at Arren, and at the mage, and at the dragon. But he did not say anything. And then the dragon spoke.

None there but Ged to whom it spoke could understand it, for dragons speak only in the Old Speech, which is their tongue. The voice was soft and hissing, almost like a cat's when he cries out softly in rage, but huge, and there was a terrible music in it. Whoever heard that voice stopped still, and listened.

The mage answered briefly, and again the dragon spoke, poising above him on slight-shifting wings: even, thought Arren, like a dragonfly poised on the air.

Then the mage answered one word, "*Memeas*," I will come; and he lifted up his staff of yew-wood. The dragon's jaws opened, and a coil of smoke escaped them in a long arabesque. The gold wings clapped like thunder, making a great wind that smelled of burning: and he wheeled and flew hugely to the north.

It was quiet on the rafts, with a little thin piping and wailing of children, and women comforting them; and men climbed aboard out of the sea somewhat shamefaced; and the forgotten torches burned in the first rays of the sun.

The mage turned to Arren. His face had a light in it that might have been joy or stark anger, but he spoke quietly. "Now we must go, lad. Say your farewells, and come." He turned to thank the chief of the raft-folk and bid him farewell, and then went from the great raft across three others, as they still lay close ingathered for the dancing, till he came to the one to which *Lookfar* was tied. So the boat had followed the raft-town in its long slow drift into the south, rocking along empty behind;

but the Children of the Open Sea had filled its empty cask with hoarded rainwater, and made up its stock of provisions, wishing thus to honour their guests; for many of them believed Sparrow-hawk to be one of the Great Ones, who had taken on the form of a man instead of the form of a whale. When Arren joined him he had the sail up. Arren loosed the rope and leapt into the boat, and in that instant she veered from the raft and her sail stiffened as in a high wind, though only the breeze of sunrise blew. She heeled turning and sped off northward on the dragon's track, light as a blown leaf on the wind.

When Arren looked back he saw the raft-town as a tiny scattering, like sticks and chips of wood afloat: the shelters and the torch-poles. Soon these were lost in the dazzle of early sunlight on the water. *Lookfar* fled forward. When her bow bit the waves, fine crystal spray flew, and the wind of her going flung back Arren's hair and made him squint.

Under no wind of earth could that small boat have sailed so fast, unless in storm, and then might have foundered in the storm-waves. This was no wind of earth, but the mage's word and power, that sent her forth so fleet.

He stood a long time by the mast, with watchful eyes. At last he sat down in his old place by the tiller, and laid one hand upon it, and looked at Arren.

"That was Orm Embar," he said, "the Dragon of Selidor, kin to that great Orm who slew Erreth-Akbe and was slain by him."

"Was he hunting, lord?" said Arren; for he was not certain whether the mage had spoken to the dragon in welcome or in threat.

"Hunting me. What dragons hunt, they find. He came to ask my help." He laughed shortly. "And that's a thing I would not believe if any told me: that a dragon turned to a man for help. And of them all, that one! He is not the oldest, though he is very old, but he is the mightiest of his kind. He does not hide his name, as dragons and men must do. He has no fear that any can gain power over him. Nor does he deceive, in the way of his kind. Long ago, on Selidor, he let me live, and he told me a great truth; he told me how the Rune of the Kings might be refound. To him I owe the Ring of Erreth-Akbe. But never did I think to repay such a debt, to such a creditor!"

"What does he ask?"

"To show me the way I seek," said the mage, more grimly. And after a pause, "He said, 'In the west there is another Dragonlord; he works destruction on us, and his power is greater than ours.' I said, 'Even than thine, Orm Embar?' and he said, 'Even than mine. I need thee: follow in haste.' And so bid, I obeyed."

"You know no more than that?"

"I will know more."

Arren coiled up the mooring line, and stowed it, and saw to other small matters about the boat, but all the while the tension of excitement sang in him like a tightened bowstring, and it sang in his voice when he spoke at last. "This is a better guide," he said, "than the others!"

Sparrowhawk looked at him, and laughed. "Aye," he said. "This time we will not go astray, I think."

So those two began their great race across the ocean. A thousand miles and more it was from the uncharted seas of the raft-folk to the island Selidor, which lies of all the lands of Earthsea the farthest west. Day after day rose shining from the clear horizon, and sank into the red west, and under the gold arch of the sun and the silver wheeling of the stars the boat ran northward, all alone on the sea.

Sometimes the thunderclouds of high summer massed far off, casting purple shadows down on the horizon; then Arren would watch the mage as he stood up and with voice and hand called those clouds to drift towards them, and to loosen their rain down on the boat. The lightning would leap among the clouds, and the thunder would bellow, and still the mage stood with upraised hand, until the rain came pouring down on him, and on Arren, and into the vessels they had set out, and into the boat, and onto the sea, flattening the waves with its violence. He and Arren would grin with pleasure, for of food they had enough if none to spare, but water they needed. And the furious splendour of the storm that obeyed the mage's word delighted them.

Arren wondered at this power which his companion now used so lightly, and once he said, "When we began our voyage, you used to work no charms."

"The first lesson on Roke, and the last, is *Do what is needful*. And no more!"

"The lessons in between, then, must consist in learning what is needful."

"They do. One must consider the Balance. But when the Balance itself is broken—then one considers other things. Above all, haste."

"But how is it that all the wizards of the South—and elsewhere by now—even the chanters of the rafts—all have lost their art, but you keep yours?"

"Because I desire nothing beyond my art," Sparrowhawk said.

And after some time he added, more cheerfully, "And if I am soon to lose it, I shall make the best of it while it lasts."

There was indeed a kind of lightheartedness in him now, a pure pleasure in his skill, which Arren, seeing him always so careful, had not guessed. The mind of the magician takes delight in tricks; a mage is a trickster. Sparrowhawk's disguise in Hort Town, which had so troubled Arren, had been a game to him; a very slight game, too, for one who could transform not just his face and voice at will, but his body and very being, becoming as he chose a fish, a dolphin, a hawk. And once he said, "Look, Arren: I'll show you Gont," and had him look at the surface of their water-cask, which he had opened, and which was full to the brim. Many simple sorcerers can cause an image to appear on the water-mirror, and so he had done: a great peak, cloud-wreathed, rising from a grey sea. Then the image changed, and Arren saw plainly a cliff of that mountain isle. It was as if he was a bird, gull or falcon, hanging on the wind off shore and looking across the wind at that cliff that towered from the breakers for two thousand feet. On the high shelf of it was a little house. "That is Re Albi," said Sparrowhawk, "and there lives my master, Ogion, he who stilled the earthquake long ago. He tends his goats, and gathers herbs, and keeps his silence. I wonder if he still walks on the mountain; he is very old now. But I would know, surely I would know, even now, if Ogion died. . . ." There was no certainty in his voice; for a moment the image wavered, as if the cliff itself were falling. It cleared, his voice cleared: "He used to go up into the forests alone, in late summer and in autumn. So he came first to me, when I was a brat in a mountain village, and gave me my name. And my life with it." The image of the water-mirror now showed as if the watcher were a bird among the forest branches, looking out to steep sunlit meadows beneath the rock and snow of the peak, looking inward along a steep road going down in a green, gold-shot darkness. "There is no silence like the silence of those forests," Sparrowhawk said, yearning.

The image faded, and there was nothing but the blinding disk of the noon sun reflected in the water in the cask.

"There," Sparrowhawk said looking at Arren with a strange, mocking look, "there, if I could ever go back there, not even you could follow me."

Land lay ahead, low and blue in the afternoon like a bank of mist. "Is it Selidor?" Arren asked, and his heart beat fast, but the mage answered, "Obb, I think, or Jessage. We're not half way yet, lad."

That night they sailed the straits between those two islands. They saw no lights, but there was a reek of smoke in the air, so heavy that their lungs grew raw with breathing it. When day came and they looked back, the eastern isle, Jessage, looked burnt and black as far as they could see inland from the shore, and a haze hung blue and dull above it.

"They have burnt the fields," Arren said.

"Aye. And the villages. I have smelled that smoke before."

"Are they savages, here in the West?"

Sparrowhawk shook his head. "Farmers; townsmen."

Arren stared at the black ruin of the land, the withered trees of orchards against the sky; and his face was hard. "What harm have the trees done them?" he said. "Must they punish the grass for their own faults? Men are savages, who would set a land afire because they have a quarrel with other men."

"They have no guidance," Sparrowhawk said. "No king; and the kingly men, and the wizardly men, all drawn aside and drawn into their own minds, hunting the door through death. So it was in the South, and so I guess it to be here."

"And this is one man's doing—the one the dragon spoke of? It seems not possible."

"Why not? If there were a King of the Isles, he would be one man. And he would rule. One man may as easily destroy, as govern: be King, or Anti-King."

There was again that note in his voice of mockery, or challenge, which roused Arren's temper.

"A king has servants, soldiers, messengers, lieutenants. He governs through his servants. Where are the servants of this— Anti-King?"

"In our minds, lad. In our minds. The traitor, the self, the self that cries *I want to live, let the world rot so long as I can live*! The little traitor soul in us, in the dark, like the spider in a box. He talks to all of us. But only some understand him. The wizards, the singers, the makers. And the heroes, the ones who

144

seek to be themselves. To be oneself is a rare thing, and a great one. To be oneself forever, is that not greater still?"

Arren looked straight at Sparrowhawk. "You mean that it is not greater. But tell me why. I was a child when I began this voyage, I did not believe in death. I have learned something, not much maybe but something, I have learned to believe in death. But I have not learned to rejoice over it, to welcome my death, or yours. If I love life shall I not hate the end of it?"

Arren's fencing-master in Berila had been a man of about sixty, short, bald, and cold. Arren had disliked him for years, though he knew him for a great swordsman. But one day in practice he had caught his master off guard and disarmed him: and he never forgot the incredulous, incongruous happiness that had suddenly gleamed in the master's cold face, the hope, the joy—an equal, at last an equal! From that day on the fencing-master had trained him mercilessly, and whenever they fenced that same relentless smile would be on the old man's face, brightening as Arren fought him harder. It was on Sparrow-hawk's face now.

"Life without end," the mage said. "Life without death. Immortality. Every soul desires it, and its health is the strength of its desire. But be careful, Arren. You are one who might achieve your desire."

"And then?"

"And then—this. This blight upon the lands. The arts of man forgotten. The singer tongueless. The eye blind. And then? A false king ruling. Ruling forever. And over the same subjects forever. No births; no new lives. No children. Only what is mortal bears life, Arren. Only in death is there rebirth. The Balance is not a stillness. It is a movement—an eternal becoming."

"But how can the Balance of the Whole be endangered by one man's acts, one man's life? Surely it is not possible, it would not be allowed—" He halted.

"Who allows? Who forbids?"

"I do not know."

"Nor I."

Almost sullenly, doggedly, Arren asked, "Then how is it you are so sure?"

"I know how much evil one man can do," Sparrowhawk said, and his scarred face frowned, but rather as if in pain than in anger. "I know it because I have done it. I have done the same evil, moved by the same pride. I opened the door between the worlds. Only a crack, a little crack, only to prove that I was stronger than death itself. I was young, and had not met death —like you. . . . It took the strength of the Archmage Nemmerle, it took his mastery and his life, to shut that door. You can see the mark that night left on me, on my face. But him it killed. Oh, the door between the light and the darkness can be opened, Arren; it takes strength, but it can be done. But to shut it again, there's a different story."

"But what you did surely was not the same—"

"Why? Because I am a good man?" That coldness like the fencer's sword was in Sparrowhawk's eye again. "What is a good man, Arren? Is a good man one who would not do evil, who would not open a door to the darkness, who has no darkness in him? Look again, lad. Look a little farther. You'll need what you learn, to go where you must go. Look into yourself! Did you not hear a voice say *Come*? Did you not follow?"

"I did. But I—I thought that voice was his."

"It was his. And it was yours. How could he speak to you, and to all those who know how to listen, but in your own voice?"

"Why do you not hear it, then?"

"Because I will not!" Sparrowhawk said fiercely. "I was born to power, even as you were. But you are young. You stand on the borders of possibility, in the shadowland, in the realm of dream, and you hear the voice saying *Come.* As I did once. But I am old. I have made my choices, I have done what I must do. I stand in daylight facing my own death. And I know that there is only one power worth having. And that is the power, not to take, but to accept. Not to have, but to give."

Jessage was far behind them now, a blue stain on the sea.

"Then I am his servant," Arren said.

"You are. And I am yours."

"But who is he, then? What is he?"

"A man, I think."

"That man you spoke of once—the sorcerer of Havnor, who summoned up the dead? Is it he?"

"It may well be."

"But he was old, you said, when you knew him years ago. . . . Would he not have died by now?"

"Maybe," Sparrowhawk said.

And they said no more.

That night the sea was full of fire. The sharp waves thrown back by *Lookfar*'s prow, and the movement of every fish through the surface water, were all outlined and alive with light. Arren sat with his arm on the gunwale and his head on his arm, watching those curves and whorls of silver radiance. He put his hand in the water and raised it again, and light ran softly from his fingers. "Look," he said, "I too am a wizard."

"That gift you have not," said his companion.

"Much good I shall be to you without it," said Arren, gazing at the restless shimmer of the waves, "when we meet our enemy."

For he had hoped—from the very beginning he had hoped—that the reason why the Archmage had chosen him and him alone for this voyage was that he had some inborn power, descended from his ancestor Morred, which would in the ultimate need and the blackest hour be revealed: and so he would save himself, and his lord, and all the world, from the enemy. But lately he had looked once more at that hope, and it was as if he saw it from a great distance; it was like remembering that, when he was a very little boy, he had had a burning desire to try on his father's crown, and had wept when he was forbidden to. This hope was as ill-timed, as childish. There was no magery in him. There never would be.

The time might come, indeed, when he could, when he must, put on his father's crown, and rule as Prince of Enlad. But that seemed a small thing now, and his home a small place, and remote. There was no disloyalty in this. Only his loyalty had grown greater, being fixed upon a greater model and a broader hope. He had learned his own weakness, also, and by it had learned to measure his strength; and he knew that he was strong. But what use was strength, if he had no gift, nothing to offer, still, to his lord, but his service and his steady love? Where they were going, would those be enough?

Sparrowhawk said only, "To see a candle's light one must take it into a dark place." With that Arren tried to comfort himself; but he did not find it very comforting.

Next morning when they woke the air was grey and the water was grey. Over the mast the sky brightened to the blue of an opal, for the fog lay low. To Northern men such as Arren of Enlad and Sparrowhawk of Gont, the fog was welcome, like an old friend. Softly it enclosed the boat so that they could not see far, and it was to them like being in a familiar room after many weeks of bright and barren space and the wind blowing. They were coming back into their own climate, and were now perhaps at the latitude of Roke.

And some seven hundred miles east of those fog-clad waters where *Lookfar* sailed, clear sunlight shone on the leaves of the trees of the Immanent Grove, on the green crown of Roke Knoll, and on the high slate roofs of the Great House.

In a room in the south tower, a magicians' workroom cluttered with retorts and alembics and great-bellied, crook-necked bottles, thick-walled furnaces and tiny heating-lamps, tongs, bellows, stands, pliers, files, pipes, a thousand boxes and vials and stoppered jugs marked with Hardic or more secret runes, and all such paraphernalia of alchemy, glass-blowing, metal-refining, and the arts of healing, in that room among the much-encumbered tables and benches stood the Master Changer and the Master Summoner of Roke.

In his hands the grey-haired Changer held a great stone like a diamond uncarved. It was a rock-crystal, coloured faintly deep within with amethyst and rose, but clear as water. Yet as the eye looked into that clarity it found unclarity, and neither reflection nor image of what was real round about, but only planes and depths ever farther, ever deeper, until it was led quite into dream and found no way out. This was the Stone of Shelieth. It had long been kept by the princes of Way, sometimes as a mere bauble of their treasury, sometimes as a charm for sleep, sometimes for a more baneful purpose: for those who looked too long and without understanding into that endless depth of crystal, might go mad. But the Archmage Gensher of Way, coming to Roke, had brought with him the Stone of Shelieth, for in the hands of a mage it held the truth.

Yet the truth varies with the man.

Therefore the Changer, holding it and looking through its bossed, uneven surface into the infinite, pale-coloured, shimmering depths, spoke aloud to tell what he saw. "I see the earth, even as though I stood on Mount Onn in the centre of the world and beheld all beneath my feet, even to the farthest isle of the farthest Reaches, and beyond. And all is clear. I see ships in the lanes of Ilien, and the hearthfires of Torheven, and the roofs of this tower where we stand now. But past Roke, nothing. In the south, no lands. In the west, no lands. I cannot see Wathort where it should be, nor any isle of the West Reach, even so close as Pendor. And Osskil and Ebosskil, where are they? There is a mist on Enlad, a greyness, like a spider's web. Each time I look more islands are gone, and the sea where they were is empty and unbroken, even as it was before the Making—" and his voice stumbled on the last word as if it came with difficulty to his lips.

He set the stone down on its ivory stand, and stood away from it. His kindly face looked drawn. He said, "Tell me what you see."

The Master Summoner took up the crystal in his hands and turned it slowly as if seeking on its rough, glassy surface an entrance of vision. A long time he handled it, his face intent. At last he set it down and said, "Changer, I see little. Fragments, glimpses, making no whole."

The grey-haired Master clenched his hands. "Is that not strange in itself?"

"How so?"

"Are your eyes often blind?" the Changer cried, as if enraged. "Do you not see that there is," and he stammered several times before he could speak, "that there is a hand upon your eyes, even as there is a hand over my mouth?"

The Summoner said, "You are overwrought, my lord."

"Summon the Presence of the Stone," said the Changer, controlling himself, but speaking somewhat stifled.

"Why?"

"Why, because I ask you."

"Come, Changer, do you dare me—like boys before a bear's den? Are we children?"

"Yes! Before what I see in the Stone of Shelieth, I am a child—a frightened child. Summon the Presence of the Stone. Must I beg you, my lord?"

"No," said the tall Master, but he frowned, and turned from the older man. Then stretching wide his arms in the great gesture that begins the spells of his art, he raised his head and spoke the syllables of invocation. As he spoke, a light grew within the Stone of Shelieth. The room darkened about it; shadows gathered. When the shadows were deep and the stone was very bright, he brought his hands together, and lifted the crystal before his face, and looked into its radiance.

He was silent some while, and then spoke. "I see the Fountains of Shelieth," he said softly. "The pools and basins and the waterfalls, the silver-curtained dripping caves where ferns grow in banks of moss, the rippled sands, the leaping up of the waters and the running of them, the outwelling of deep springs from earth, the mystery and sweetness of the source, the spring. . . ." He fell silent again, and stood so for a time, his face pale as silver in the light of the stone. Then he cried aloud wordlessly, and dropping the crystal with a crash fell to his knees, his face hidden in his hands.

There were no shadows. Summer sunlight filled the jumbled room. The great stone lay beneath a table in the dust and litter, unharmed.

The Summoner reached out blindly, catching at the other man's hand like a child. He drew a deep breath. At last he got up, leaning a little on the Changer, and said with unsteady lips and some attempt to smile, "I will not take your dares again, my lord."

"What saw you, Thorion?"

"I saw the fountains. I saw them sink down, and the streams run dry, and the lips of the springs of water draw back. And underneath all was black, and dry. You saw the sea before the Making, but I saw the . . . what comes after . . . I saw the Unmaking." He wet his lips. "I wish that the Archmage were here," he said.

"I wish that we were there with him."

"Where? There is none that can find him now." The Summoner looked up at the windows that showed the blue, untroubled sky. "No sending can come to him, no summoning reach him. He is there where you saw an empty sea. He is coming to the place where the springs run dry. He is where our arts do not avail. . . . Yet maybe even now there are spells that might reach to him, some of those in the Lore of Paln."

"But those are spells whereby the dead are brought among the living."

"Some bring the living among the dead."

"You do not think him dead?"

"I think he goes towards death, and is drawn towards it. And so are we all. Our power is going from us, and our strength, and our hope and luck. The springs are running dry."

The Changer gazed at him a while with a troubled face. "Do not seek to send to him, Thorion," he said at last. "He knew what he sought long before we knew it. To him the world is even as this Stone of Shelieth: he looks and sees what is and what must be. . . . We cannot help him. The great spells have grown very perilous, and of all there is most danger in the Lore of which you spoke. We must stand fast as he bade us, and look to the walls of Roke, and the remembering of the Names."

"Aye," said the Summoner. "But I must go and think on this." And he left the tower room, walking somewhat stiffly and holding his noble, dark head high.

In the morning the Changer sought him. Entering his room after vain knocking, he found him stretched asprawl on the stone floor, as if he had been hurled backward by a heavy blow. His arms were flung wide as if in the gesture of invocation, but his hands were cold, and his open eyes saw nothing. Though the Changer knelt by him and called him with a mage's authority, saying his name, Thorion, thrice over, yet he lay still. He was not dead, but there was in him only so much life as kept his heart beating very slowly, and a little breath in his lungs. The Changer took his hands, and holding them whispered, "O Thorion, I forced you to look into the Stone. This is my doing!" Then going hastily from the room he said aloud to those he met, Masters and students, "The enemy has reached among us, into Roke the well-defended, and has stricken our strength at its heart!" Though he was a gentle man, he looked so fey and cold that those who saw him feared him. "Look to the Master Summoner," he said. "Though who will summon back his spirit? since he the master of his art is gone."

He went towards his own chamber, and they all drew back to let him pass.

The Master Healer was sent for. He had them lay Thorion the Summoner abed, and cover him warmly; but he brewed no herb of healing, nor did he sing any of the chants that aid the sick body or the troubled mind. One of his pupils was with him, a young boy not yet made sorcerer, but promising in the arts of healing, and he asked, "Master, is there nothing to be done for him?"

"Not on this side of the wall," said the Master Healer. Then, recalling to whom he spoke, he said, "He is not ill, lad; but even if this were a fever or illness of the body, I do not know if our craft would much avail. It seems there is no savour in my herbs of late; and though I say the words of our spells, there is no virtue in them."

"That is like what the Master Chanter said yesterday. He stopped in the middle of a song he was teaching us, and said, 'I do not know what the song means.' And he walked out of the room. Some of the boys laughed, but I felt as if the floor had sunk out from under me."

The Healer looked at the boy's blunt, clever face, and then down at the Summoner's face, cold and rigid. "He will come back to us," he said. "The songs will not be forgotten."

But that night the Changer went from Roke. No one saw the manner of his going. He slept in a room with a window looking out into a garden; the window was open in the morning, and he was gone. They thought he had transformed himself, with his own skill of form-change, into a bird or beast, or a mist or wind even, for no shape or substance was beyond his art, and so had fled from Roke, perhaps to seek for the Archmage. Some, knowing how the shape-changer may be caught in his own spells if there is any failure of skill or will, feared for him, but they said nothing of their fears.

So there were three of the Masters lost to the Council of the Wise. As the days passed and no news ever came of the Archmage, and the Summoner lay like one dead, and the Changer did not return, a chill and gloom grew in the Great House. The boys whispered among themselves, and some of them spoke of leaving Roke, for they were not being taught what they had come to learn. "Maybe," said one, "they were all lies from the beginning, these secret arts and powers. Of the Masters, only the Master Hand still does his tricks, and these, we all know, are frank illusion. And now the others hide, or refuse to do anything, because their tricks have been revealed." Another, listening, said, "Well, what is wizardry? What is this art magic, beyond a show of seeming? Has it ever saved a man from death, or given long life, even? Surely if the mages have the power they claim to have, they'd all live forever!" And he and the other boy fell to telling over the deaths of the great mages, how Morred had been killed in battle, and Nereger by the Grey Mage, and Erreth-Akbe by a dragon, and Gensher, the last Archmage, by mere sickness, in his bed, like any man. Some of the boys listened gladly, having envious hearts; others listened and were wretched.

All this time the Master Patterner stayed alone in the Grove, and let none enter it.

But the Doorkeeper, though seldom seen, was not changed. He bore no shadow in his eyes. He smiled, and kept the doors of the Great House against its lord's return.

10 *The Dragons' Run*

On the seas of the outermost West Reach that Lord of the Island of the Wise, waking cramped and stiff in a small boat in a cold, bright morning, sat up and yawned. And after a moment, pointing north, he said to his yawning companion, "There! Two islands, do you see them? The southmost of the isles of the Dragons' Run."

"You have a hawk's eyes, lord," said Arren, peering through sleep over the sea, and seeing nothing.

"Therefore I am the Sparrowhawk," the mage said; he was still cheerful, seeming to shrug off forethought and foreboding. "Can't you see them?"

"I see gulls," said Arren, after rubbing his eyes and searching all the blue-grey horizon before the boat.

The mage laughed. "Could even a hawk see gulls at twenty miles' distance?"

As the sun brightened above the eastern mists, the tiny wheeling flecks in the air that Arren watched seemed to sparkle, like gold-dust shaken in water, or dust-motes in a sunbeam. And then Arren realised that they were dragons.

As *Lookfar* approached the islands Arren saw the dragons soaring and circling on the morning wind, and his heart leapt up with them with a joy, a joy of fulfilment, that was like pain.

All the glory of mortality was in that flight. Their beauty was made up of terrible strength, and utter wildness, and the grace of reason. For these were thinking creatures, with speech, and ancient wisdom: in the patterns of their flight there was a fierce, willed concord.

Arren did not speak, but he thought: I do not care what comes after; I have seen the dragons on the wind of morning.

At times the patterns jarred, and the circles broke, and often in flight one dragon or another would jet from its nostrils a long streak of fire that curved and hung on the air a moment repeating the curve and brightness of the dragon's long, arching body. Seeing that, the mage said, "They are angry. They dance their anger on the wind."

And presently he said, "Now we're in the hornet's nest." For the dragons had seen the little sail on the waves, and first one, then another, broke from the whirlwind of their dancing and came stretched long and level on the air, rowing with great wings, straight towards the boat.

The mage looked at Arren, who sat at the tiller, since the waves ran rough and counter. The boy held it steady with a steady hand, though his eyes were on the beating of those wings. As if satisfied, Sparrowhawk turned again, and standing by the mast, let the magewind drop from the sail. He lifted up his staff and spoke aloud.

At the sound of his voice and the words of the Old Speech, some of the dragons wheeled in mid-flight, scattering, and returned to the isles. Others halted and hovered, the sword-like claws of their forearms outstretched but checked. One, dropping low over the water, flew slowly on towards them: in two wing-strokes it was over the boat. The mailed belly scarcely cleared the mast. Arren saw the wrinkled, unarmoured flesh between the inner shoulder-joint and breast, which, with the eye, is the dragon's only vulnerable part, unless the spear that strikes be mightily enchanted. The smoke that rolled from the long, toothed mouth choked him, and with it came a carrion stench that made him wince and retch.

The shadow passed. It returned, as low as before, and this time Arren felt the furnace-blast of breath before the smoke. He heard Sparrowhawk's voice, clear and fierce. The dragon passed over. Then all were gone, streaming back to the isles like fiery cinders on a gust of wind.

Arren caught his breath, and wiped his forehead, which was covered with cold sweat. Looking at his companion he saw his hair had gone white: the dragon's breath had burnt and crisped the ends of the hairs. And the heavy cloth of the sail was scorched brown along one side.

"Your head is somewhat singed, lad."

"So is yours, lord."

Sparrowhawk passed his hand over his hair, surprised. "So it is!—That was an insolence; but I seek no quarrel with these creatures. They seem mad, or bewildered. They did not speak. Never have I met a dragon who did not speak before it struck, if only to torment its prey. . . . Now we must go forward. Do not look them in the eye, Arren. Turn aside your face if you must. We'll go with the world's wind, it blows fair from the south, and I may need my art for other things. Hold her as she goes."

Lookfar moved forward and soon had on her left a distant island, and on her right the twin isles they had seen first. These rose up into low cliffs, and all the stark rock was whitened with the droppings of the dragons and of the little black-headed terns that nested fearlessly amongst them.

The dragons had flown up high, and circled in the upper air as vultures circle. Not one stooped down again to the boat. Sometimes they cried out to one another, high and harsh across the gulfs of air, but if there were words in their crying Arren could not make them out.

The boat rounded a short promontory, and he saw on the

shore what he took for a moment to be a ruined fortress. It was a dragon. One black wing was bent under it and the other stretched out vast across the sand and into the water, so that the come and go of waves moved it a little to and fro in a mockery of flight. The long snake-body lay full length on the rock and sand. One foreleg was missing, and the armour and flesh were torn from the great arch of the ribs, and the belly was torn open, so that the sand for yards about was blackened with the poisoned dragon-blood. Yet the creature still lived. So great a life is in dragons that only an equal power of wizardry can kill them swiftly. The green-gold eyes were open, and as the boat sailed by, the lean, huge head moved a little, and with a rattling hiss steam mixed with bloody spray shot from the nostrils.

The beach between the dying dragon and the sea's edge was tracked and scored by the feet and heavy bodies of its kind, and its entrails were trodden into the sand.

Neither Arren nor Sparrowhawk spoke until they were well clear of that island and heading across the choppy, restless channel of the Dragons' Run, full of reefs and pinnacles and shapes of rock, towards the northern islands of the double chain. Then Sparrowhawk said, "That was an evil sight," and his voice was bleak and cold.

"Do they . . . eat their own kind?"

"No. No more than we do. They have been driven mad. Their speech has been taken from them. They who spoke before men spoke, they who are older than any living thing, the Children of Segoy,—they have been driven to the dumb terror of the beasts. Ah! Kalessin! where have your wings borne you? Have you lived to see your race learn shame?" His voice rang like struck iron, and he looked upward, searching the sky. But the dragons were behind, circling lower now above the rocky isles and the blood-stained beach, and overhead was nothing but the blue sky and the sun of noon.

There was then no man living who had sailed the Dragons'

Run, or seen it, except the Archmage. Twenty years ago and more, he had sailed the length of it from east to west and back again. It was a nightmare and a marvel, to a sailor. The water was a maze of blue channels and green shoals, and among these, by hand and word and most vigilant care, he and Arren now picked their boat's way, between the rocks and reefs. Some of these lay low, under or half-under the wash of the waves, covered with anemone and barnacle and ribbony seafern; like water-monsters, shelled or sinuous. Others stood up in cliff and pinnacle sheer from the sea, and there were arches and half-arches, carven towers, fantastic shapes of animals, boars' backs and serpents' heads, all huge, deformed, diffuse, as if life writhed half-conscious in the rock. The sea-waves beat on them with a sound like breathing, and they were wet with the bright, bitter spray. In one such rock from the south there was plainly visible the hunched shoulders and heavy, noble head of a man, stooped in pondering thought above the sea; but when the boat had passed it, looking back from the north, all man was gone from it and the massive rocks revealed a cave in which the sea rose and fell making a hollow, clapping thunder; and there seemed to be a word, a syllable, in that sound. As they sailed on, the garbling echoes lessened and this syllable came more clearly; so that Arren said, "Is there a voice in the cave?"

"The sea's voice."

"But it speaks a word."

Sparrowhawk listened; he glanced at Arren, and back at the cave. "How do you hear it?"

"As saying the sound *ahm*."

"In the Old Speech that signifies the beginning, or long ago. But I hear it as *ohb*, which is a way of saying the end.—Look ahead there!" he ended abruptly, even as Arren warned him, "Shoal water!" And, though *Lookfar* picked her way like a cat among the dangers, they were busy with the steering for some while, and slowly the cave forever thundering out its enigmatic word fell behind them.

Now the water deepened and they came out from among the phantasmagoria of the rocks; and ahead of them loomed an island like a tower. Its cliffs were black, and made up of many cylinders or great pillars pressed together, with straight edges and plane surfaces, rising three hundred feet sheer from the water.

"That is the Keep of Kalessin," said the mage. "So the dragons named it to me, when I was here long ago."

"Who is Kalessin?"

"The eldest. . . ."

"Did he build this place?"

"I do not know. I don't know if it was built. Nor how old he is. I say 'he', but I do not even know that. . . . To Kalessin, Orm Embar is like a yearling kid. And you and I are like may-flies." He scanned the terrific palisades, and Arren looked up at them uneasily, thinking how a dragon might drop from that far, black rim and be upon them almost with its shadow. But no dragon came. They passed slowly through the still waters in the lee of the rock, hearing nothing but the whisper and clap of shadowed waves on the columns of basalt. The water here was deep, without reef or rock; Arren handled the boat, and Sparrowhawk stood up in the prow, searching the cliffs and the bright sky ahead.

The boat passed out at last from the shadow of the Keep of Kalessin into the sunlight of late afternoon. They were across the Dragon's Run. The mage lifted his head, like one who sees what he had looked to see, and across that great space of gold before them came on golden wings the dragon Orm Embar.

Arren heard Sparrowhawk's cry to him: *Aro Kalessin?* He guessed the meaning of that, but could make no sense of what the dragon answered. Yet hearing the Old Speech he felt always that he was on the point of understanding, almost understanding: as if it were a language he had forgotten, not one he had never known. In speaking it the mage's voice was much clearer than when he spoke Hardic, and seemed to make a kind of silence about it, as does the softest touch on a great bell. But the dragon's voice was like a gong, both deep and shrill, or the hissing thrum of cymbals.

Arren watched his companion stand there in the narrow prow, speaking with the monstrous creature that hovered above him filling half the sky; and a kind of rejoicing pride came into the boy's heart, to see how small a thing a man is, how frail, and how terrible. For the dragon could have torn the man's head from his shoulders with one stroke of his taloned foot, he could have crushed and sunk the boat as a stone sinks a floating leaf, if it were only size that mattered. But Sparrowhawk was as dangerous as Orm Embar: and the dragon knew it.

The mage turned his head. "Lebannen," he said, and the boy got up and came forward, though he wanted to go not one boat's length, not one step, closer to those fifteen-foot jaws and the long, slit-pupilled, yellow-green eyes that burned upon him from the air.

Sparrowhawk said nothing to him, but put a hand on his shoulder, and spoke again to the dragon, briefly.

"Lebannen," said the vast voice with no passion in it. "*Agni* Lebannen!"

He looked up; the pressure of the mage's hand reminded him, and he avoided the gaze of the green-gold eyes.

He could not speak the Old Speech; but he was not dumb. "I greet thee, Orm Embar, Lord Dragon," he said clearly, as one prince greets another.

Then there was a silence, and Arren's heart beat hard and laboured. But Sparrowhawk, standing by him, smiled.

After that the dragon spoke again, and Sparrowhawk replied; and this seemed long to Arren. At last it was over, and suddenly. The dragon sprang aloft with a wingbeat that all but heeled the boat over, and was off. Arren looked at the sun, and found it seemed no nearer setting than before; the time had not really been long. But the mage's face was the colour of wet ashes, and his eyes glittered as he turned to Arren. He sat down on the thwart.

"Well done, lad," he said hoarsely. "It is not easy—talking to dragons."

Arren got them food, for they had not eaten all day; and the mage said no more until they had eaten and drunk. By then the sun was low to the horizon, though in these northern latitudes, and not long past midsummer, night came late and slowly.

"Well," he said at last, "Orm Embar has, after his fashion, told me much. He says that the one we seek is, and is not, on Selidor. . . . It is hard for a dragon to speak plainly. They do not have plain minds. And even when one of them would speak the truth to a man, which is seldom, he does not know how truth looks to a man. So I asked him, 'Even as thy father Orm is on Selidor?' For as you know, there Orm and Erreth-Akbe died in their battle. And he answered, 'No and yes. You will find him on Selidor, but not on Selidor.' " Sparrowhawk paused and pondered, chewing on a crust of hardbread. "Maybe he meant that though the man is not on Selidor, yet I must go there to get to him. Maybe. . . . I asked him then of the other dragons. He said that this man has been among them, having no fear of them, for though killed he re-arises from death, in his body, alive. Therefore they fear him as a creature outside nature; and their fear gives his wizardry hold over them, and he takes the Speech of the Making from them, leaving them prey to their own wild nature. So they devour one another, or take their own lives, plunging into the sea—a loathly death for the fire-serpent, the beast of wind and fire. Then I said, 'Where is their lord Kalessin?' and all he would answer was, 'In the West,' which might mean that Kalessin has flown away to the other lands which dragons say lie farther than ever ship has sailed; or it may not mean that. So then I ceased my questions, and he asked his, saying, "I flew over Kaltuel returning north, and over the Toringates. On Kaltuel I saw villagers killing a baby on an altar stone, and on Ingat I saw a sorcerer killed by his townsfolk throwing stones at him. Will they eat the baby, think you, Ged? Will the sorcerer come back from death and throw stones at his townsfolk?' I thought he mocked me, and was about to speak in anger, but he was not mocking. He said, 'The sense has gone out of things. There is a hole in the world and the sea is running out of it. The light is running out. We will be left in the dry land. There will be no more speaking, and no more dying.' So at last I saw what he would say to me."

Arren did not see it; and moreover was sorely troubled. For Sparrowhawk, in repeating the dragon's words, had named himself by his own true name, unmistakably. This brought unwelcome into Arren's mind the memory of that tormented woman of Lorbanery crying out, "My name is Akaren!" If the powers of wizardry, and of music, and speech, and trust, were weakening and withering among men, if an insanity of fear was coming on them so that, like the dragons bereft of reason, they turned on each other to destroy: if all this were so, would his lord escape it? Was he so strong?

He did not look strong, sitting hunched over his supper of bread and smoked fish, with hair greyed and fire-singed, and slight hands, and a tired face.

Yet the dragon feared him.

"What irks you, lad?"

Only the truth would do, with him.

"My lord, you spoke your name."

"Oh, aye. I forgot I had not done so earlier. You will need my true name, if we go where we must go." He looked up, chewing, at Arren. "Did you think I grew senile, and went about babbling my name, like old bleared men past sense and shame? Not yet, lad!"

"No," said Arren, so confused that he could say nothing else. He was very weary; the day had been long, and full of dragons. And the way ahead grew dark.

"Arren," said the mage—"No: Lebannen: where we go, there is no hiding. There all bear their own true names."

"The dead cannot be hurt," said Arren sombrely.

"But it is not only there, not in death only, that men take their names. Those who can be most hurt, the most vulnerable: those who have given love, and do not take it back: they speak each other's names. The faithful-hearted, the givers of life. . . . You are worn out, lad. Lie down and sleep. There's nothing to do now but keep the course all night. And by morning we shall see the last island of the world."

In his voice was an insuperable gentleness. Arren curled up in the prow, and sleep began to come into him at once. He heard the mage begin a soft, almost whispering chant, not in the Hardic tongue but in the words of the Making; and as he began to understand at last, and to remember what the words meant, just before he understood them, he fell fast asleep.

Silently the mage stowed away their bread and meat, looked to the lines, made all trim in the boat, and then, taking the guide-line of the sail in hand and sitting down on the after thwart, he set the magewind strong in the sail. Tireless, *Lookfar* sped north, an arrow over the sea.

He looked down at Arren. The boy's sleeping face was lit redgold by the long sunset, the rough hair was wind-stirred. The soft, easy, princely look of the boy who had sat by the fountain of the Great House a few months since was gone; this was a thinner face, and harder, and much stronger. But it was not less beautiful.

"I have found none to follow in my way," Ged the Archmage said aloud to the sleeping boy or to the empty wind. "None but thee. And thou must go thy way, not mine. Yet will thy kingship be, in part, my own. For I knew thee first. I knew thee first!

They will praise me more for that in afterdays than for anything I did of magery. . . . If there will be afterdays. For first we two must stand upon the balance-point, the very fulcrum of the world. And if I fall, you fall, and all the rest. . . . For a while, for a while. No darkness lasts forever. And even there, there are stars. . . . Oh, but I should like to see thee crowned in Havnor, and the sunlight shining on the Tower of the Sword, and on the Ring we brought for thee from Atuan, from the dark tombs, Tenar and I, before ever thou wast born!"

He laughed then, and turning to face the north, he said to himself, in the common tongue, "A goatherd to set the heir of Morred on his throne! Will I never learn?"

Presently, as he sat with the guide-rope in his hand and watched the full sail strain reddened in the last light of the west, he spoke again softly. "Not in Havnor would I be, and not in Roke. It is time to be done with power. To drop the old toys, and go on. It is time that I went home. I would see Tenar. I would see Ogion, and speak with him before he dies, in the house on the cliffs of Re Albi. I crave to walk on the mountain, the mountain of Gont, in the forests, in the autumn when the leaves are bright. There is no kingdom like the forests. It is time I went there, went in silence, went alone. And maybe there I would learn at last what no act, or art, or power can teach me, what I have never learned."

The whole west blazed up in a fury and glory of red, so that the sea was crimson and the sail above it bright as blood; and then the night came quietly on. All that night long the boy slept and the man waked, gazing forward steadily into the dark. There were no stars.

11   *Selidor*

Waking in the morning Arren saw before the boat, dim and low along the blue west, the shores of Selidor.

In the Hall in Berila were old maps that had been made in the days of the Kings, when traders and explorers had sailed from the Inner Lands and the Reaches had been better known. A great map of the North and West was laid in mosaic on two walls of the Prince's throne-room, with the isle of Enlad in gold and grey above the throne; and Arren saw it in his mind's eye as he had seen it a thousand times in boyhood. North of Enlad was Osskil, and west of it Ebosskil, and south of that Semel and Paln; and there the Inner Lands ended, and there was nothing but the pale blue-green mosaic of the empty sea, set here and there with a tiny dolphin or a whale. Then at last, after the corner where the north wall met the west wall, there was Narveduen, and beyond it three lesser islands. And then the empty sea again, on and on; until the very edge of the wall, and the end of the map, and there was Selidor, and beyond it, nothing.

He could recall it vividly, the curving shape of it, with a great bay in the heart of it, opening narrowly to the east. They had not come so far north as that, but were steering now for a deep cove in the southernmost cape of the island, and there, while the sun was still low in the haze of morning, they came to land.

So ended their great run from the Roads of Balatran to the Western Isle. The stillness of the earth was strange to them, when they had beached *Lookfar*, and walked after so long on solid ground.

Ged climbed a low dune, grass-crowned, the crest of it leaning out over the steep slope, bound into cornices by the tough roots of the grass. When he reached the summit he stood still, looking west and north. Arren stopped at the boat to put on his shoes, which he had not worn for many days, and he took his sword out of the gear-box and buckled it on, this time with no questions in his mind as to whether or not he should do so. Then he climbed up beside Ged to look at the land.

The dunes ran inland, low and grassy, for half a mile or so, and then there were lagoons, thick with sedge and salt-reeds, and beyond those, low hills lay yellow-brown and empty out of sight. Beautiful and desolate was Selidor. Nowhere on it was there any mark of man, his work or habitation. There were no beasts to be seen, and the reed-filled lakes bore no flocks of gulls or wild geese or any bird.

They descended the inland side of the dune, and the slope of sand cut off the noise of the breakers and the sound of the wind, so that it became still.

Between the outmost dune and the next was a dell of clean sand, sheltered, the morning sun shining warm on its western slope. "Lebannen," the mage said, for he used Arren's true name now, "I could not sleep last night, and now I must. Stay with me and keep watch." He lay down in the sunlight, for the shade was cold; put his arm over his eyes; sighed, and slept. Arren sat down beside him. He could see nothing but the white slopes of the dell, and the dune-grass bowing at the top against the misty blue of the sky, and the yellow sun. There was no sound except the muted murmur of the surf, and sometimes the wind gusting moved the particles of sand a little with a faint whispering.

Arren saw what might have been an eagle flying very high, but it was not an eagle. It circled and stooped, and down it came with that thunder and shrill whistle of outspread golden wings. It alighted on huge talons on the summit of the dune. Against the sun the great head was black, with fiery glints.

The dragon crawled a little way down the slope, and spoke. "Agni Lebannen," it said.

Standing between it and Ged, Arren answered: "Orm Embar." And he held his bare sword in his hand.

It did not feel heavy, now. The smooth, worn hilt was comfortable in his hand; it fitted. The blade had come lightly, eagerly, from the sheath. The power of it, the age of it, were on his side, for he knew now what use to make of it. It was his sword.

The dragon spoke again, but Arren could not understand. He glanced back at his sleeping companion, whom all the rush and thunder had not awakened, and said to the dragon, "My lord is weary; he sleeps."

At that Orm Embar crawled and coiled on down to the bottom of the dell. He was heavy on the ground, not lithe and free as when he flew, but there was a sinister grace in the slow placing of his great taloned feet and the curving of his thorny tail. Once there he drew his legs beneath him, lifted up his huge head, and was still: like a dragon carved on a warrior's helm. Arren was aware of his yellow eye, not ten feet away, and of the faint reek of burning that hung about him. This was no carrion stink; dry and metallic, it accorded with the faint odours of the sea and the salt sand, a cleanly, wild smell.

The sun rising higher struck the flanks of Orm Embar, and he burned like a dragon made of iron and gold.

Still Ged slept, relaxed, taking no more notice of the dragon than a sleeping farmer of his hound.

So an hour passed, and Arren, starting, found the mage had sat up beside him.

"Have you got so used to dragons that you fall asleep between their paws?" said Ged, and laughed, and yawned. Then rising he spoke to Orm Embar in the dragons' speech.

Before Orm Embar answered, he too yawned—perhaps in sleepiness, perhaps in rivalry—and that was a sight that few have lived to remember: the rows of yellow-white teeth as long and sharp as swords, the forked, red, fiery tongue twice the length of a man's body, the fuming cavern of the throat.

Orm Embar spoke, and Ged was about to answer, when both turned to look at Arren. They had heard, clear in the silence, the hollow whisper of steel on sheath. Arren was looking up at the lip of the dune behind the mage's head, and his sword was ready in his hand.

There stood, bright lit by sunlight, the faint wind stirring his garments slightly, a man. He stood still as a carven figure except for that flutter of the hem and hood of his light cloak. His hair was long and black, falling in a mass of glossy curls; he was broad-shouldered and tall, a strong, comely man. His eyes seemed to look out over them, at the sea. He smiled.

"Orm Embar I know," he said. "And you also I know, though you have grown old since I last saw you, Sparrowhawk. You are Archmage now, they tell me. You have grown great, as well as old. And you have a young servant with you: a prentice mage, no doubt, one of those who learn wisdom on the Isle of the Wise. What do you two here, so far from Roke and the invulnerable walls that protect the Masters from all harm?"

"There is a breach in greater walls than those," said Ged, clasping both hands on his staff and looking up at the man. "But will you not come to us in the flesh, so that we may greet one whom we have long sought?"

"In the flesh?" said the man, and smiled again. "Is mere

flesh, body, butcher's meat, of such account between two mages? No, let us meet mind to mind, Archmage."

"That, I think, we cannot do.—Lad, put up your sword. It is but a sending, an appearance, no true man. As well draw blade against the wind.—In Havnor, when your hair was white, you were called Cob. But that was only a use-name. How shall we call you when we meet you?"

"You will call me Lord," said the tall figure on the dune's edge.

"Aye, and what else?"

"King and Master."

At that Orm Embar hissed, a loud and hideous sound, and his great eyes gleamed; yet he turned his head away from the man, and sank crouching in his tracks, as if he could not move.

"And where shall we come to you, and when?"

"In my domain, and at my pleasure."

"Very well," said Ged, and lifting up his staff moved it a little towards the tall man—and the man was gone, like a candle-flame blown out.

Arren stared, and the dragon rose up mightily on his four crooked legs, his mail clanking and the lips writhing back from his teeth. But the mage leaned on his staff again.

"It was only a sending. A presentment or image of the man. It can speak and hear, but there's no power in it, save what our fear may lend it. Nor is it even true in seeming, unless the sender so wishes. We have not seen what he now looks like, I guess."

"Is he near, do you think?"

"Sendings do not cross water. He is on Selidor. But Selidor is a great island: broader than Roke or Gont, and near as long as Enlad. We may seek him long."

Then the dragon spoke. Ged listened, and turned to Arren. "Thus says the Lord of Selidor: 'I have come back to my own land, nor will I leave it. I will find the Unmaker and bring you to him, that together we may abolish him.' And have I not said that what a dragon hunts, he finds?"

Thereupon Ged went down on one knee before the great creature, as a liegeman kneels before a king, and thanked him in his own tongue. The breath of the dragon, so close, was hot on his bowed head.

Orm Embar dragged his scaly weight up the dune once more, and beat his wings, and took the air.

Ged brushed the sand from his clothes, and said to Arren, "Now you have seen me kneel. And maybe you'll see me kneel once more, before the end."

Arren did not ask what he meant; in their long companionship he had learned that there was reason in the mage's reserve. Yet it seemed to him that there was evil omen in the words.

They crossed over the dune to the beach once more to make sure the boat lay high above the reach of tide or storm, and to take from her cloaks for the night and what food they had left. Ged paused a minute by the slender prow which had borne him over strange seas so long, so far; he laid his hand on it, but he set no spell and said no word. Then they struck inland, northward, once again, towards the hills.

They walked all day, and at evening camped by a stream that wound down towards the reed-choked lakes and marshes. Though it was full summer the wind blew chill, coming from the west, from the endless landless reaches of the open sea. A mist veiled the sky, and no stars shone above the hills on which no hearth-fire or window-light had ever gleamed.

In the darkness Arren woke. Their small fire was dead, but a westering moon lit the land with a grey misty light. In the stream-valley and on the hillside about it stood a great multitude of people, all still, all silent, their faces turned towards Ged and Arren. Their eyes caught no light of the moon.

Arren dared not speak, but he put his hand on Ged's arm.

The mage stirred, and sat up saying, "What's the matter?" He followed Arren's gaze, and saw the silent people.

They were all clothed darkly, men and women alike. Their faces could not be clearly seen in the faint light, but it seemed to Arren that among those who stood nearest them in the valley, across the little stream, there were some whom he knew, though he could not say their names.

Ged stood up, the cloak falling from him. His face and hair and shirt shone silvery pale, as if the moonlight gathered itself to him. He held out his arm in a wide gesture and said aloud, "O you who have lived, go free! I break the bond that holds you: *Anvassa mane harw pennodathe!*"

For a moment they stood still, the multitude of silent people. They turned away slowly, and seemed to walk into the grey darkness, and were gone.

Ged sat down. He drew a deep breath. He looked at Arren, and put his hand on the boy's shoulder, and his touch was warm and firm. "There's nothing to fear, Lebannen," he said, gently, mockingly. "They were only the dead."

Arren nodded, though his teeth were chattering and he felt cold to his very bones. "How did," he began, but his jaw and lips would not obey him yet.

Ged understood him. "They came at his summoning. This is what he promises: eternal life. At his word they may return. At his bidding they must walk upon the hills of life, though they cannot stir a blade of grass."

"Is he—is he then dead, too?"

Ged shook his head, brooding. "The dead cannot summon the dead back into the world. No, he has the powers of a living man; and more. . . . But if any thought to follow him, he tricked them. He keeps his power for himself. He plays King of the Dead; and not only of the dead. . . . But they were only shadows."

"I don't know why I fear them," Arren said with shame.

"You fear them because you fear death, and rightly: for death is terrible, and must be feared," the mage said. He laid new wood on the fire, and blew on the small coals under the ashes. A little flare of brightness bloomed on the twigs of brushwood, a grateful light to Arren. "And life also is a terrible thing," Ged said, "and must be feared, and praised."

They both sat back, wrapping their cloaks close about them. They were silent a while. Then Ged spoke very gravely. "Lebannen, how long he may tease us here with sendings and with shadows, I do not know. But you know where he will go at last."

"Into the dark land."

"Aye. Among them."

"I have seen them now. I will go with you."

"Is it faith in me that moves you? You may trust my love, but do not trust my strength. For I think I have met my match."

"I will go with you."

"But if I am defeated, if my power or my life is spent, I cannot guide you back; you cannot return alone."

"I will return with you."

At that Ged said, "You enter your manhood at the gate of death." And then he said that word or name by which the dragon had twice called Arren, speaking it very low: "Agni— Agni Lebannen."

After that they spoke no more, and presently sleep came back into them, and they lay down by their small and briefly-burning fire.

The next morning they walked on, going north and west; this was Arren's decision, not Ged's, who said, "Choose us our way, lad; the ways are all alike to me." They made no haste, for they had no goal, waiting for some sign from Orm Embar. They followed the lowest, outermost range of hills, mostly within sight of the ocean. The grass was dry and short, blowing and blowing for ever in the wind. The hills rose up golden and forlorn upon their right, and on their left lay the salt marshes and the western sea. Once they saw swans flying, far away in the south. No other breathing creature did they see all that day. A kind of weariness of dread, of waiting for the worst, grew in Arren all day long. Impatience and a dull anger rose in him. He said after hours of silence, "This land is as dead as the land of death itself!"

"Do not say that," the mage said sharply. He strode on a while and then went on, in a changed voice, "Look at this land; look about you. This is your kingdom, the kingdom of life. This is your immortality. Look at the hills, the mortal hills. They do not endure forever. The hills with the living grass on them, and the streams of water running. . . . In all the world, in all the worlds, in all the immensity of time, there is no other like each of those streams, rising cold out of the earth where no eye sees it, running through the sunlight and the darkness to the sea. Deep are the springs of being, deeper than life, than death...."

He stopped, but in his eyes as he looked at Arren and at the sunlit hills there was a great, wordless, grieving love. And Arren saw that, and seeing it saw him, saw him for the first time whole, as he was.

"I cannot say what I mean," Ged said unhappily.

But Arren thought of that first hour in the Fountain Court, of the man who had knelt by the running water of the fountain; and joy, as clear as that remembered water, welled up in him. He looked at his companion and said, "I have given my love to what is worthy of love. Is that not the kingdom, and the unperishing spring?"

"Aye, lad," said Ged, gently, and with pain.

They went on together in silence. But Arren saw the world now with his companion's eyes, and saw the living splendour that was revealed about them in the silent, desolate land, as if by a power of enchantment surpassing any other, in every blade of the wind-bowed grass, every shadow, every stone. So when one stands in a cherished place for the last time before a voyage without return, he sees it all whole, and real, and dear, as he has never seen it before and never will see it again.

As evening came on serried lines of clouds rose from the west, borne on great winds from the sea, and burned fiery before the sun, reddening it as it sank. As he gathered brushwood for their fire in a creek-valley, in that red light, Arren glanced up and saw a man standing not ten feet from him. The man's face looked vague and strange, but Arren knew him, the Dyer of Lorbanery, Sopli, who was dead.

Behind him stood others, all with sad, staring faces. They seemed to speak, but Arren could not hear their words, only a kind of whispering blown away by the west wind. Some of them came towards him slowly.

He stood and looked at them, and again at Sopli; and then he turned his back on them, and stooped, and picked up one more stick of brushwood, though his hands shook. He added it to his load, and picked up another, and one more. Then he straightened, and looked back. There was no one in the valley, only the red light burning on the grass. He returned to Ged, and set down his load of firewood, but he said nothing of what he had seen.

All that night, in the misty darkness of that land empty of living souls, when he woke from fitful sleep he heard about him the whispering of the souls of the dead. He steadied his will, and did not listen, and slept again.

Both he and Ged woke late, when the sun, already a hand's breadth above the hills, broke free at last from fog and brightened the cold land. As they ate their small morning meal the dragon came, wheeling above them in the air. Fire shot from his jaws, and smoke and sparks from his red nostrils; his teeth gleamed like blades of ivory in that lurid glare. But he said nothing, though Ged hailed him, crying in his language, "Hast found him, Orm Embar?"

The dragon threw back his head and arched his body strangely, raking the wind with his razor talons. Then he set off flying fast to the west, looking back at them as he went.

Ged gripped his staff, and struck it on the ground. "He cannot speak," he said. "He cannot speak! The words of the Making are taken from him, and he is left like an adder, like a tongueless worm, his wisdom dumb. Yet he can lead, and we can follow!" Swinging up their light packs on their backs they strode westward across the hills as Orm Embar had flown.

Eight miles or more they went, not slackening that first swift steady pace. Now the sea lay on either hand, and they walked on a long, falling ridge-back that ran down at last through dry reeds and winding creek-beds to an outcurving beach of sand, coloured like ivory. This was the westernmost cape of all the lands, the end of earth.

Orm Embar crouched on that ivory sand, his head low like an angry cat's and his breath coming in gasps of fire. Some way before him, between him and the long, low breakers of the sea, stood a thing like a hut or shelter, white, as if built of long-bleached driftwood. But there was no driftwood on this shore which faced no other land. As they came closer Arren saw that the ramshackle walls were built up of great bones: whales' bones, he thought at first, and then saw the white triangles edged like knives, and knew they were the bones of a dragon.

They came to the place. Sunlight on the sea glittered through crevices between the bones. The lintel of the doorway was a thighbone longer than a man. On it stood a human skull, staring with hollow eyes at the hills of Selidor.

They stopped there, and as they looked up at the skull a man came out of the doorway under it. He wore an armour of gilt bronze, in an ancient fashion; it was rent as if by hatchet blows, and the jewelled scabbard of his sword was empty. His face was stern, with arched black brows and narrow nose; his eyes were dark, keen, and sorrowful. There were wounds on his arms, and in his throat and side; they bled no longer, but they were mortal wounds. He stood erect and still, and looked at them.

Ged took one step towards him. They were somewhat alike, thus face to face.

"Thou are Erreth-Akbe," Ged said. The other gazed at him steadily, and nodded once, but did not speak.

"Even thou, even thou must do his bidding." Rage was in Ged's voice. "O my lord, and best and bravest of us all, rest in thy honour and in death!" And raising his hands Ged brought them down in a great gesture, saying again those words he had spoken to the multitudes of the dead. His hands left behind on the air a moment a broad bright track. When it was gone the armoured man was gone, and only the sun dazzled on the sand where he had stood.

Ged struck at the house of bones with his staff, and it fell and vanished away. Nothing of it was left but one great rib-bone that stuck up out of the sand.

He turned to Orm Embar. "Is it here, Orm Embar? Is this the place?"

The dragon opened his mouth and made a huge gasping hiss.

"Here on the last shore of the world. That is well!" Then holding his black yew staff in his left hand, Ged opened his arms in the gesture of invocation, and spoke. Though he spoke in the language of the Making, yet Arren understood, at last, as all who hear that invocation must understand, for it has power over all: "Now do I summon you and here, my enemy, before my eyes and in the flesh, and bind you by the word that will not be spoken till time's end, to come!"

But where the name of him summoned should have been spoken, Ged said only: *My enemy*.

A silence followed, as if the sound of the sea had faded. It seemed to Arren that the sun failed and dimmed, though it stood high in a clear sky. A darkness came over the beach, as though one looked through smoked glass; directly before Ged it grew very dark, and it was hard to see what was there. It was as if nothing was there, nothing the light could fall on, a formlessness.

Out of it came a man, suddenly. It was the same man they had seen upon the dune, black-haired and long-armed, lithe and tall. He held now a long rod or blade of steel, graven all down its length with runes, and he tilted this towards Ged as he faced him. But there was something strange in the look of his eyes, as if they were sun-dazzled and could not see.

"I come," he said, "at my own choosing, in my own way. You cannot summon me, Archmage. I am no shadow. I am alive. I only am alive! You think you are, but you are dying, dying. Do you know what this is I hold? It is the staff of the Grey Mage; he who silenced Nereger; the Master of my art. But I am the Master now. And I have had enough of playing games with you." With that he suddenly reached out the steel blade to touch Ged, who stood as if he could not move, and could not speak. Arren stood a pace behind him, and all his will was to move, but he could not stir, he could not even put his hand on his sword-hilt, and his voice was stopped in his throat.

But over Ged and Arren, over their heads, vast and fiery, the great body of the dragon came in one writhing leap, and plunged down full force upon the other, so that the charmed steel blade entered into the dragon's mailed breast to its full length: but the man was borne down under his weight and crushed and burned.

Rising up again from the sand, arching his back and beating his vaned wings, Orm Embar vomited out gouts of fire, and screamed. He tried to fly, but he could not fly. Malign and cold, the metal lay in his heart. He crouched, and the blood ran black and poisonous, steaming, from his mouth, and the fire died in his nostrils till they became like pits of ash. He laid down his great head on the sand.

So died Orm Embar where his forefather Orm died, on the bones of Orm buried in the sand.

But where he had struck his enemy to earth, there lay something ugly and shrivelled, like the body of a big spider dried up in its web. It had been burned by the dragon's breath, and crushed by his taloned feet. Yet, as Arren watched, it moved. It crawled away a little from the dragon.

The face lifted up towards them. There was no comeliness left in it, only ruin, old age that had outlived old age. The mouth was withered. The sockets of the eyes were empty, and had long been empty. So Ged and Arren saw at last the living face of their enemy.

It turned away. The burnt, blackened arms reached out, and a darkness gathered into them, that same shapeless darkness that swelled and dimmed the sunlight. Between the arms of the Unmaker it was like an archway or a gate, though dim and without outline; and through it was neither pale sand nor ocean, but a long slope of darkness going down into the dark.

There the crushed, crawling figure went, and when it came into the darkness it seemed suddenly to rise up, and move swiftly, and it was gone.

"Come, Lebannen," said Ged, laying his right hand on the boy's arm, and they went forward into the dry land.

12   The Dry Land

The yew-wood staff in the mage's hand shone in the dull, lowering darkness with a silver gleam. Another slight glimmering movement caught Arren's eye: a flicker of light along the blade of the sword he held naked in his hand. As the dragon's act and death broke the binding spell, he had drawn his sword, there on the beach of Selidor. And here, though he was no more than a shadow, he was a living shadow, and bore the shadow of his sword.

There was no other brightness anywhere. It was like a late twilight under clouds at the end of November, a dour, chill, dull air in which one could see, but not clearly and not far. Arren knew the place, the moors and barrens of his hopeless dreams; but it seemed to him that he was farther, immensely farther, than he had ever been in dream. He could make out nothing distinctly, except that he and his companion stood on the slope of a hill, and before them was a low wall of stones, no higher than a man's knee.

Ged still kept his right hand on Arren's arm. He moved forward now, and Arren went with him; they stepped over the wall of stones.

Formless, the long slope fell away before them, descending into the dark.

But overhead, where Arren had thought to see a heavy overcast of cloud, the sky was black, and there were stars. He looked at them, and it seemed as if his heart shrank small and cold within him. They were no stars that he had ever seen. Unmoving they shone, unwinking. They were those stars that do not rise, nor set, nor are they ever hidden by any cloud, nor does any sunrise dim them. Still and small they shine on the dry land.

Ged set off walking down the far side of the hill of being, and pace by pace Arren went with him. There was terror in him, and yet so resolved was his heart and so intent his will that the fear did not rule him, nor was he even very clearly aware of it; only it was as if something deep within him grieved, like an animal shut up in a room and chained.

It seemed that they walked down that hill-slope for a long way, but perhaps it was a short way; for there was no passing of time there, where no wind blew and the stars did not move. They came then into the streets of one of the cities that are there, and Arren saw the houses with windows that are never lit, and in certain doorways standing, with quiet faces and empty hands, the dead.

The market places were all empty. There was no buying and selling there, no gaining and spending. Nothing was used; nothing was made. Ged and Arren went through the narrow streets alone, though a few times they saw a figure at the turning of another way, distant and hardly to be seen in the gloom. At sight of the first of these Arren started and raised his sword to point, but Ged shook his head and went on. Arren saw then that the figure was a woman, who moved slowly, not fleeing from them.

All those whom they saw—not many, for the dead are many, but that land is large—stood still, or moved slowly and with no purpose. None of them bore wounds, as had the semblance of Erreth-Akbe summoned into daylight at the place of his death.

No marks of illness were on them. They were whole, and healed. They were healed of pain, and of life. They were not loathesome as Arren had feared they would be, not frightening in the way he had thought they would be. Quiet were their faces, freed from anger and desire, and there was in their shadowed eyes no hope.

Instead of fear, then, great pity rose up in Arren, and if fear underlay it, it was not for himself, but for us all. For he saw the mother and child who had died together, and they were in the dark land together; but the child did not run, nor did it cry, and the mother did not hold it, nor ever look at it. And those who had died for love passed each other in the streets.

The potter's wheel was still, the loom empty, the stove cold. No voice ever sang.

The dark streets between dark houses led on and on, and they passed through them. The sound of their feet was the only sound. It was cold. Arren had not noticed that cold at first, but it crept into his spirit, which was, here, also his flesh. He felt very weary. They must have come a long way. Why go on? he thought, and his steps lagged a little.

Ged stopped suddenly, turning to face a man who stood at the crossing of two streets. He was slender and tall, with a face that Arren thought he had seen, but could not remember where. Ged spoke to him, and no other voice had broken the silence since they stepped across the wall of stones: "O Thorion, my friend, how come you here!"

And he put out his hands to the Summoner of Roke.

Thorion made no answering gesture. He stood still, and his face was still; but the silvery light on Ged's staff struck deep in his enshadowed eyes, making a little light there, or meeting it. Ged took the hand he did not offer, and said again, "What do you here, Thorion? You are not of this kingdom yet. Go back!"

"I followed the undying one. I lost my way." The

Summoner's voice was soft and dull, like that of a man who speaks in sleep.

"Upward: towards the wall," said Ged, pointing the way he and Arren had come, the long, dark, descending street. At that there was a tremor in Thorion's face, as if some hope had entered into him like a sword, intolerable.

"I cannot find the way," he said. "My lord, I cannot find the way."

"Maybe thou shalt," Ged said, and embraced him, and then went forward. Thorion stood still at the crossroads, behind him.

As they went on it seemed to Arren that in this timeless dusk there was, in truth, neither forward nor back, no east nor west, no way to go. Was there a way out? He thought how they had come down the hill, always descending, no matter how they turned; and still in the dark city the streets went downward, so that to return to the wall of stones they need only climb, and at the hill's top they would find it. But they did not turn. Side by side, they went on. Did he follow Ged? Or did he lead him?

They came out of the city. The country of the innumerable dead was empty. No tree or thorn or blade of grass grew in the stony earth under the unsetting stars.

There was no horizon, for the eye could not see so far into the gloom; but ahead of them the small, still stars were absent from the sky over a long space above the ground, and this starless space was jagged and sloped like a chain of mountains. As they went on the shapes were more distinct: high peaks, weathered by no wind or rain. There was no snow on them to gleam in starlight. They were black. The sight of them struck desolation into Arren's heart. He looked away from them. But he knew them; he recognised them; his eyes were drawn back to them. Each time he looked at those peaks he felt a cold weight in his breast, and his nerve came near to failing. Still he walked on, always downward, for the land fell away, descending towards

the mountains' feet. At last he said, "My lord, what are. . . ."
He pointed at the mountains, for he could not go on speaking;
his throat was dry.

"They border on the world of light," Ged answered, "even
as does the wall of stones. They have no name but Pain. There
is a road across them. It is forbidden to the dead. It is not long.
But it is a bitter road."

"I am thirsty," Arren said, and his companion answered,
"Here they drink dust."

They went on.

It seemed to Arren that his companion's gait had slowed
somewhat, and sometimes he hesitated. He himself felt no more
hesitation, though the weariness had not ceased to grow in him.
They must go down, they must go on. They went on.

Sometimes they passed through other towns of the dead,
where the dark roofs made angles against the stars, which stood
forever in the same place above them. After the towns was the
empty land again, where nothing grew. As soon as they had
come out of a town, it was lost in the darkness. Nothing could
be seen, before or behind, except the mountains that grew ever
nearer, towering before them. To their right the formless slope
fell away as it had done, how long ago? when they crossed the
wall of stones. "What lies that way?" Arren murmured to Ged,
for he craved the sound of speech, but the mage shook his head:
"I do not know. It may be a way without an end."

In the direction they went the slope seemed to be growing
less, and always less. The ground under their feet gritted
harshly, like lava-dust. Still they went on, and now Arren
never thought of returning, or of how they might return. Nor
did he think of stopping, though he was very weary. Once he
tried to lighten the numb darkness and weariness and horror
within him by thinking of his home; but he could not remember
what sunlight looked like, nor his mother's face. There was
nothing to do but to go on. And he went on.

He felt the ground level under his feet; and beside him Ged hesitated. Then he too stopped. The long descent was over; this was the end; there was no way further, no need to go on.

They were in the valley directly under the Mountains of Pain. There were rocks underfoot, and boulders about them, rough to the touch like scoria, as if this narrow valley might be the dry bed of a river of water that had once run here, or the course of a river of fire long since cold, from the volcanoes that reared their black, unmerciful peaks above.

He stood still, there in the narrow valley in the dark, and Ged stood still beside him. They stood like the aimless dead, gazing at nothing, silent. Arren thought, with a little dread but not much, "We have come too far."

It did not seem to matter much.

Speaking his thought, Ged said, "We have come too far to turn back." His voice was soft, but the ring of it was not wholly muted by the great gloomy hollowness around them, and at the sound of it Arren roused a little. Had they not come here to meet the one they sought?

A voice in the darkness said, "You have come too far."

Arren answered it, saying, "Only too far is far enough."

"You have come to the Dry River," said the voice. "You cannot go back to the wall of stones. You cannot go back to life."

"Not that way," said Ged, speaking into the darkness. Arren could hardly see him, though they stood side by side, for the mountains under which they stood cut out half the starlight, and it seemed as if the current of the Dry River was darkness itself. "But we would learn your way."

There was no answer.

"We meet as equals here. If you are blind, Cob, yet we are in the dark."

There was no answer.

"We cannot hurt you here; we cannot kill you. What is there to fear?"

"I have no fear," said the voice in the darkness. Then slowly, glimmering a little as with that light that sometimes clung to Ged's staff, the man appeared standing some way upstream from Ged and Arren, among the great dim masses of the boulders. He was tall, broad-shouldered and long-armed, like that figure which had appeared to them on the dune and on the beach of Selidor, but older; the hair was white, and thickly matted over the high forehead. So he appeared in the spirit, in the kingdom of death, not burnt by the dragon's fire, not maimed; but not whole. The sockets of his eyes were empty.

"I have no fear," he said. "What should a dead man fear?" He laughed. The sound of laughter rang so false and uncanny, there in that narrow stony valley under the mountains, that Arren's breath failed him for a moment. But he gripped his sword, and listened.

"I do not know what a dead man should fear," Ged answered. "Surely not death? Yet it seems you fear it. For you have found a way to escape from it."

"I have. I live: my body lives."

"Not well," the mage said dryly. "Illusion might hide age; but Orm Embar was not gentle with that body."

"I can mend it. I know secrets of healing and of youth, no mere illusions. What do you take me for? Because you are called Archmage, do you take me for a village sorcerer? I who alone among all mages found the Way of Immortality, which no other ever found!"

"Maybe we did not seek it," said Ged.

"You sought it. All of you. You sought it and could not find it, and so made wise words about acceptance and balance and the equilibrium of life and death. But they were words—lies to cover your failure—to cover your fear of death! What man would not live forever, if he could? And I can. I am immortal.

I did what you could not do, and therefore I am your master: and you know it. Would you know how I did it, Archmage?"

"I would."

Cob came a step closer. Arren noticed that, though the man had no eyes, his manner was not quite that of the stone-blind; he seemed to know exactly where Ged and Arren stood, and to be aware of both of them, though he never turned his head to Arren. Some wizardly second-sight he might have, such as that hearing and seeing which sendings and presentments had: something which gave him an awareness, though it might not be true sight.

"I was in Paln," he said to Ged, "after you, in your pride, thought you had humbled me and taught me a lesson. Oh, a lesson you taught me, indeed, but not the one you meant to teach! There I said to myself: I have seen death now, and I will not accept it. Let all stupid nature go its stupid course, but I am a man, better than nature, above nature. I will not go that way, I will not cease to be myself! And so determined, I took the Pelnish Lore again, but found only hints and smatterings of what I needed. So I rewove it and remade it, and made a spell—the greatest spell that has ever been made. The greatest and the last!"

"In working that spell, you died."

"Yes! I died. I had the courage to die, to find what you cowards could never find—the way back from death. I opened the door that had been shut since the beginning of time. And now I come freely to this place, and freely return to the world of the living. Alone of all men in all time I am Lord of the Two Lands. And the door I opened is open not only here, but in the minds of the living, in the depths and unknown places of their being, where we are all one in the darkness. They know it, and they come to me. And the dead too must come to me, all of them, for I have not lost the magery of the living: they must climb over the wall of stones when I bid them, all the souls, the lords, the mages, the proud women; back and forth from life to death, at my command. All must come to me, the living and the dead, I who died and live!"

"Where do they come to you, Cob? Where is that you are?"

"Between the worlds."

"But that is neither life nor death. What is life, Cob?"

"Power."

"What is love?"

"Power," the blind man repeated heavily, hunching up his shoulders.

"What is light?"

"Darkness!"

"What is your name?"

"I have none."

"All in this land bear their true name."

"Tell me yours, then!"

"I am named Ged. And you?"

The blind man hesitated, and said, "Cob."

"That was your use-name, not your name. Where is your name? Where is the truth of you? Did you leave it in Paln where you died? You have forgotten much, O Lord of the Two Lands. You have forgotten light, and love, and your own name."

"I have your name now, and power over you, Ged the Archmage—Ged who was Archmage when he was alive!"

"My name is no use to you," Ged said. "You have no power over me at all. I am a living man; my body lies on the beach of Selidor, under the sun, on the turning earth. And when that body dies, I will be here: but only in name, in name alone, in shadow. Do you not understand? Did you never understand, you who called up so many shadows from the dead, who summoned all the hosts of the perished, even my lord Erreth-Akbe, wisest of us all? Did you not understand that he, even he, is but a shadow and a name? His death did not diminish life. Nor did it diminish him. He is there—*there*, not here! Here is nothing, dust and shadows. There, he is the earth and sunlight, the leaves of trees, the eagle's flight. He is alive. And all who ever died, live; they are reborn, and have no end, nor will there ever be an end. All, save you. For you would not have death. You lost death, you lost life, in order to save yourself. Yourself! Your immortal self! What is it? Who are you?"

"I am myself. My body will not decay and die—"

"A living body suffers pain, Cob; a living body grows old; it dies. Death is the price we pay for our life, and for all life."

"I do not pay it! I can die and in that moment live again! I cannot be killed, I am immortal, I alone am myself for ever!"

"Who are you, then?"

"The Immortal One."

"Say your name."

"The King."

"Say my name. I told it to you but a minute since. Say my name!"

"You are not real. You have no name. Only I exist."

"You exist, without name, without form. You cannot see the light of day; you cannot see the dark. You sold the green earth and the sun and stars to save yourself. But you have no self. All that which you sold, that is yourself. You have given everything for nothing. And so now you seek to draw the world to you, all that light and life you lost, to fill up your nothingness. But it cannot be filled. Not all the songs of earth, not all the stars of heaven, could fill your emptiness."

Ged's voice rang like iron, there in the cold valley under the mountains, and the blind man cringed away from him. He lifted up his face, and the dim starlight shone on it; he looked as if he wept, but he had no tears, having no eyes. His mouth opened and shut, full of darkness, but no words came out of it, only a groaning. At last he said one word, barely shaping it with his contorted lips, and the word was "Life".

"I would give you life if I could, Cob. But I cannot. You are dead. But I can give you death."

"No!" the blind man screamed aloud, and then he said, "No, no," and crouched down sobbing, though his cheeks were as dry as the stony river-course where only night, and no water, ran. "You cannot. No one can ever set me free. I opened the door between the worlds, and I cannot shut it. No one can shut it. It will never be shut again. It draws, it draws me. I must come back to it. I must go through it, and come back here, into the dust and cold and silence. It sucks at me and sucks at me. I cannot leave it. I cannot close it. It will suck all the light out of the world in the end. All the rivers will be like the Dry River. There is no power anywhere that can close the door I opened!"

Very strange was the mixture of despair and vindictiveness, terror and vanity, in his words and voice.

Ged said only, "Where is it?"

"That way. Not far. You can go there. But you cannot do anything there. You cannot shut it. If you spent all your power in that one act, it would not be enough. Nothing is enough."

"Maybe," Ged answered. "Though you chose despair, remember we have not yet done so. Take us there."

The blind man raised his face, in which fear and hatred struggled visibly. Hatred triumphed. "I will not," he said.

At that Arren stepped forward, and he said, "You will."

The blind man held still. The cold silence and the darkness of the realm of the dead surrounded them, surrounded their words.

"Who are you?"

"My name is Lebannen."

Ged spoke: "You who call yourself King, do you not know who this is?"

Again Cob held utterly still. Then he said, gasping a little as he spoke, "But he is dead—You are dead. You cannot go back. There is no way out. You are caught here!" As he spoke the glimmer of light died away from him, and they heard him turn in the darkness and go away from them into it, hastily. "Give me light, my lord!" Arren cried, and Ged held up his staff above his head, letting the white light break open that old darkness, full of rocks and shadows, among which the tall, stooped figure of the blind man hurried and dodged, going upstream from them with a strange, unseeing, unhesitating gait. After him Arren came, sword in hand; and after him, Ged.

Soon Arren had outdistanced his companion, and the light was very faint, much interrupted by the boulders and the turnings of the riverbed; but the sound of Cob's going, the sense of his presence ahead, was guide enough. He drew closer, slowly, as the way became steeper. They were climbing in a steep gorge choked with stones; the Dry River, narrowing to its head, wound between sheer banks. Rocks clattered under their feet, and under their hands, for they must clamber. Arren sensed the final narrowing in of the banks, and with a lunge forward came up to Cob and caught his arm, halting him there: a kind of basin of rocks five or six feet wide, what might have been a pool if ever water ran there; and above it a tumbled cliff of rock and slag. In that cliff there was a black hole, the source of the Dry River.

Cob did not try to pull away from him. He stood quite still, while the light of Ged's approach brightened on his eyeless face. He had turned that face to Arren. "This is the place," he said at last, a kind of smile forming on his lips. "This is the place you seek. See it? There you can be reborn. All you need do is follow me. You will live immortally. We shall be kings together."

Arren looked at that dry, dark springhead, the mouth of dust, the place where a dead soul, crawling into earth and darkness, was born again dead: abominable it was to him, and he said in a harsh voice, struggling with deadly sickness, "Let it be shut!"

"It will be shut," Ged said, coming beside them: and the light blazed up now from his hands and face as if he were a star fallen on earth in that endless night. Before him the dry spring, the door yawned open. It was wide, and hollow, but whether deep or shallow there was no telling. There was nothing in it for the light to fall on, for the eye to see. It was void. Through it was neither light nor dark, neither life nor death. It was nothing. It was a way that led nowhere.

Ged raised up his hands and spoke.

Arren still held Cob's arm; the blind man had laid his free hand against the rocks of the cliff-wall. Both stood still, caught in the power of the spell.

With all the skill of his life's training, and with all the strength of his fierce heart, Ged strove to shut that door, to make the world whole once more. And under his voice and the command of his shaping hands the rocks drew together, painfully, trying to be whole, to meet; they drew together. But at the same time the light weakened and weakened, dying out from his hands and from his face, dying out from his yew staff, until only a little glimmer of it clung there. By that faint light Arren saw that the door was nearly closed.

Under his hand the blind man felt the rocks move, felt them come together: and felt also the art and power giving itself up, spending itself, spent—And all at once he shouted, "No!" and broke from Arren's grasp, lunged forward and caught Ged in his blind powerful grasp. Bearing Ged down under his weight he closed his hands on his throat to strangle him.

Arren raised up the sword of Serriadh, and brought the blade down straight and hard on the bowed neck beneath the matted hair.

The living spirit has weight in the world of the dead, and

the shadow of his sword has an edge. The blade made a great wound, severing Cob's spine. Black blood leapt out lit by the sword's own light.

But there is no good in killing a dead man; and Cob was dead, years dead. The wound closed, swallowing its blood. The blind man stood up very tall, groping out with his long arms at Arren, his face writhing with rage and hatred: as if he had just now perceived who his true enemy and rival was.

So horrible to see was this recovery from a deathblow, this inability to die, more horrible than any dying, that a rage of loathing swelled up in Arren, a berserk fury, and swinging up the sword he struck again with it, a full terrible downward blow. Cob fell with skull split open and face masked with blood, yet Arren was upon him at once, to strike again, before the wound could close, to strike until he killed. . . .

Beside him Ged, struggling to his knees, spoke one word.

At the sound of his voice Arren was stopped, as if a hand had grasped his sword-arm. The blind man, who had begun to rise, also held utterly still. Ged got to his feet; he swayed a little. When he could hold himself erect he faced the cliff.

"Be thou made whole!" he said in a clear voice, and with his staff he drew in lines of fire across the gate of rocks a figure: the rune Agnen, the rune of Ending, which closes roads and is drawn on coffin lids. And there was then no gap or void place among the boulders. The door was shut.

The earth of the Dry Land trembled under their feet, and across the unchanging, barren sky a long roll of thunder ran, and died away.

"By the word that will not be spoken until time's end I summoned thee. By the word that was spoken at the making of things I now release thee. Go free!" And bending over the blind man, who was crouched on his knees, Ged whispered in his ear, under the white tangled hair.

Cob stood up. He looked about him slowly, with seeing eyes.

He looked at Arren, and then at Ged. He spoke no word, but gazed at them with dark eyes. There was no anger in his face, no hate, no grief. Slowly he turned, and went off down the course of the Dry River, and soon was gone to sight.

There was no more light on Ged's yew-staff, nor in his face. He stood there in the darkness. When Arren came to him he caught at the young man's arm to hold himself upright. For a moment a spasm of dry sobbing shook him. "It is done," he said. "It is all gone."

"It is done, dear lord. We must go."

"Aye. We must go home."

Ged was like one bewildered or exhausted. He followed Arren back down the rivercourse, stumbling along with difficulty and slowly among the rocks and boulders. Arren stayed with him. When the banks of the Dry River were low and the ground was less steep, he turned towards the way they had come, the long, formless slope that led up into the dark. Then he turned away.

Ged said nothing. As soon as they halted he had sunk down sitting on a lava-boulder, forspent, his head hanging.

Arren knew that the way they had come was closed to them. They could only go on. They must go all the way. Even too far is not far enough, he thought. He looked up at the black peaks, cold and silent against the unmoving stars, terrible; and once more that ironic, mocking voice of his will spoke in him, unrelenting: "Will you stop halfway, Lebannen?"

He went to Ged and said very gently, "We must go on, my lord."

Ged said nothing, but he stood up.

"We must go by the mountains, I think."

"Thy way, lad," Ged said in a hoarse whisper. "Help me."

So they set out up the slopes of dust and scoria into the mountains, Arren helping his companion along as well as he could. It was black dark in the combes and gorges, so that he had to feel the way ahead, and it was hard for him to give Ged support at the same time. Walking was hard, a stumbling matter; but when they had to climb and clamber as the slopes grew steeper, that was harder still. The rocks were rough, burning the hands like molten iron. Yet it was cold, and got colder as they went higher. There was a torment in the touch of this earth. It seared like live coals: a fire burned within the mountains. But the air was always cold, and always dark. There was no sound. No wind blew. The sharp rocks broke under their hands, gave way under their feet. Black and sheer the spurs and chasms went up in front of them and fell away beside them into blackness. Behind, below, the kingdom of the dead was lost. Ahead, above, the peaks and rocks stood out against the stars. And nothing moved in all the length and breadth of those black mountains, except the two mortal souls.

Ged often stumbled or missed his footing, in weariness. His breath came harder and harder, and when his hands came hard against the rocks he gasped in pain. To hear him cry out thus wrung Arren's heart. He tried to keep him from falling. But often the way was too narrow for them to go abreast, or Arren had to go in front to seek out footing. And at last, on a high slope that ran up to the stars, Ged slipped and fell forward, and did not get up.

"My lord," Arren said, kneeling by him, and then spoke his name: "Ged."

He did not move or answer.

Arren lifted him in his arms and carried him up that high slope. At the end of it there was level ground for some way ahead. Arren laid his burden down, and dropped down beside him, exhausted and in pain, past hope. This was the summit of the pass between the two black peaks, for which he had been struggling. This was the pass, and the end. There was no way farther. The end of the level ground was the edge of a cliff: beyond it the darkness went on forever, and the small stars hung unmoving in the black gulf of the sky.

Endurance may outlast hope. He crawled forward, when he was able to do so, doggedly. He looked over the edge of darkness. And below him, only a little way below, he saw the beach of ivory sand; the white and amber waves were curling and breaking in foam on it, and across the sea the sun was setting in a haze of gold.

Arren turned back to the dark. He went back. He lifted Ged up as best he could, and struggled forward with him until he could not go any farther. There all things ceased to be: thirst, and pain, and the dark, and the sun's light, and the sound of the breaking sea.

13   The Stone of Pain

When Arren woke a grey fog hid the sea and the dunes and hills of Selidor. The breakers came murmuring in a low thunder out of the fog and withdrew murmuring into it again. The tide was in, and the beach much narrower than when they had first come there; the last small foam-lines of the waves came and licked at Ged's outflung left hand as he lay face down on the sand. His clothes and hair were wet, and Arren's clothes clung icy to his body, as if once at least the sea had broken over them. Of Cob's dead body there was no trace. Maybe the waves had drawn it out to sea. But behind Arren, when he turned his head, huge and dim in the mist the grey body of Orm Embar bulked like a ruined tower.

Arren got up, shuddering with chill; he could barely stand, for cold, and stiffness, and a dizzy weakness like that which comes of lying a long time unmoving. He staggered like a drunken man. As soon as he could control his limbs he went to Ged and managed to pull him a little way up the sand above the waves' reach, but that was all he could do. Very cold, very heavy, Ged seemed to him; he had borne him over the boundary from death into life, but maybe in vain. He put his ear to Ged's breast, but could not still the shaking in his own limbs and the chattering of his teeth to listen for the heartbeat. He stood up again, and tried to stamp to bring some warmth back into his legs, and finally, trembling and dragging his legs like an old man, set off to find their packs. They had dropped them beside a little stream running down from the ridge of the hills, a long time ago, when they came down to the house of bones. It was that stream he sought, for he could not think of anything but water, fresh water.

Before he expected it he came to the stream, as it descended onto the beach and wandered mazy and branching like a tree of silver to the sea's edge. There he dropped down and drank, with his face in the water, and his hands in the water, sucking up the water into his mouth and into his spirit.

At last he sat up, and as he did so he saw on the far side of the stream, immense, a dragon.

Its head, the colour of iron, stained as with red rust at nostril and eye socket and jowl, hung facing him, almost over him. The talons sank deep into the soft wet sand on the edge of the stream. The folded wings were partly visible, like sails, but the length of the dark body was lost in the fog.

It did not move. It might have been crouching there for hours, or for years, or for centuries. It was carven of iron, shaped from rock—but the eyes, the eyes he dared not look into, the eyes like oil coiling on water, like yellow smoke behind glass, the opaque, profound, and yellow eyes watched Arren.

There was nothing he could do; so he stood up. If the dragon would kill him, it would; and if it did not, he would try to help Ged, if there was any help for him. He stood up, and started to walk up the rivulet to find their packs.

The dragon did nothing. It crouched unmoving, and watched. Arren found the packs, and filled both the skin bottles at the stream, and went back across the sand to Ged. After he had taken only a few steps away from the stream, the dragon was lost in the thick fog.

He gave Ged water, but could not rouse him. He lay lax and

cold, his head heavy on Arren's arm. His dark face was greyish, the nose and cheek-bones and the old scar standing out harshly. Even his body looked thin and burned, as if half consumed.

Arren sat there on the damp sand, his companion's head on his knees. The fog made a vague soft sphere about them, lighter overhead. Somewhere in the fog was the dead dragon Orm Embar, and the live dragon waiting by the stream. And somewhere across Selidor the boat *Lookfar*, with no provisions in her, lay on another beach. And then the sea, eastward. Three hundred miles to any other land of the West Reach, maybe; a thousand to the Inmost Sea. A long way. "As far as Selidor," they used to say on Enlad. The old stories told to children, the myths, began, "As long ago as forever and as far away as Selidor, there lived a prince. . . ."

He was the prince. But in the old stories, that was the beginning; and this seemed to be the end.

He was not downcast. Though very tired, and grieving for his companion, he felt not the least bitterness of regret. Only there was no longer anything he could do. It had all been done.

When his strength came back into him, he thought, he would try surf-fishing with the line from his pack; for once his thirst was quenched he had begun to feel the gnawing of hunger, and their food was gone, all but one packet of hardbread. He would save that, for if he soaked and softened it in water he might be able to feed some of it to Ged.

And that was all there was left to do. Beyond that he could not see; the mist was all about him.

He felt about in his pockets as he sat there, huddled with Ged in the fog, to see if he had anything useful. In his tunic pocket was a hard, sharp-edged thing. He drew it forth and looked at it, puzzled. It was a small stone, black, porous, hard. He almost tossed it away. Then he felt the edges of it in his hand, rough and searing, and felt the weight of it, and knew

it for what it was, a bit of rock from the Mountains of Pain.
It had caught in his pocket as he climbed or when he crawled
to the edge of the pass with Ged. He held it in his hand, the
unchanging thing, the stone of pain. He closed his hand on it,
and held it. And he smiled then, a smile both sombre and
joyous, knowing, for the first time in his life, and alone, and
unpraised, and at the end of the world, victory.

The mists thinned and moved. Far out through them he saw
sunlight on the open sea. The dunes and hills came and went,
colourless and enlarged by the veils of fog. Sunlight struck
bright on the body of Orm Embar, magnificent in death.

The iron-black dragon crouched, never moving, on the far
side of the stream.

Past noon the sun grew clear and warm, burning the last
blur of mist out of the air. Arren threw off his wet clothes and
let them dry, and went naked save for his sword-belt and sword.
He let the sun dry Ged's clothing likewise, but though the
great healing comfortable flood of heat and light poured down
on Ged, yet he lay still.

There was a noise as of metal rubbing against metal, the
grating whisper of crossed swords. The iron-coloured dragon
had risen on its crooked legs. It moved, and crossed the rivulet,
with a soft hissing sound as it dragged its long body through
the sand. Arren saw the wrinkles at the shoulder joints, and
the mail of the flanks scored and scarred like the armour of
Erreth-Akbe, and the long teeth yellowed and blunt. In all
this, and in its sure, ponderous movements, and in a deep
and frightening calmness that it had, he saw the sign of age:
of great age, of years beyond remembering. So when the dragon
stopped some few feet from where Ged lay, and Arren stood
up between the two, he said, in Hardic for he did not know
the Old Speech, "Art thou Kalessin?"

The dragon said no word, but it seemed to smile. Then,

lowering its huge head and sticking out its neck, it looked down at Ged, and spoke his name.

Its voice was huge, and soft, and smelt like a blacksmith's forge.

Again it spoke, and once more; and at the third time, Ged opened his eyes. After a while he tried to sit up, but could not. Arren knelt by him and supported him. Then Ged spoke. "Kalessin," he said, "*senvanissai'n ar Roke!*" He had no more strength after speaking; he leaned his head on Arren's shoulder and shut his eyes.

The dragon made no reply. It crouched as before, not moving. The fog was coming in again, dimming the sun as it went down to the sea.

Arren dressed, and wrapped Ged in his cloak. The tide which had drawn far out was coming in again, and he thought to carry his companion up to dryer ground on the dunes, for he felt his strength coming back.

But as he bent to lift Ged up, the dragon put out a great, mailed foot, almost touching him. The talons of that foot were four, with a spur behind such as a cock's foot has, but these were spurs of steel, and as long as scythe-blades.

"*Sobriost,*" said the dragon, like a January wind through frozen reeds.

"Let my lord be. He has saved us all, and doing so has spent his strength, and maybe his life with it. Let him be!"

So Arren spoke, fiercely and with command. He had been overawed and frightened too much, he had been filled up with fear, and had got sick of it and would not have it any more. He was angry with the dragon for its brute strength and size, its unjust advantage. He had seen death, he had tasted death, and no threat had power over him.

The old dragon Kalessin looked at him from one long, awful, golden eye. There were ages beyond ages in the depths of that eye; the morning of the world was deep in it. Though Arren did not look into it, he knew that it looked upon him with profound and mild hilarity.

"*Arw sobriost*," said the dragon, and its rusty nostrils widened so that the banked and stifled fire deep within them glittered.

Arren had his arm under Ged's shoulders, having been in the act of lifting him when Kalessin's movement stopped him, and now he felt Ged's head turn a little, and heard his voice: "It means, mount here."

For a while Arren did not move. This was all folly. But there was the great taloned foot, set like a step in front of him; and above it, the crook of the elbow joint; and above that, the jutting shoulder, and the musculature of the wing where it sprang from the shoulder-blade: four steps; a stairway. And there in front of the wings and the first great iron thorn of the spine-armour, in the hollow of the neck there was place for a man to sit astride, or two men. If they were mad, and past hope, and given up to folly.

"Mount!" said Kalessin in the speech of the Making.

So Arren stood up and helped his companion to stand. Ged held his head erect, and with Arren's arms to guide him climbed up those strange steps. Both sat down astride in the rough-mailed hollow of the dragon's neck, Arren behind, ready to support Ged if he needed it. Both felt a warmth come into them, a welcome heat like the sun's heat, where they touched the dragon's hide: life burned in fire beneath that iron armour.

Arren saw that they had left the mage's staff of yew lying half-buried in the sand; the sea was creeping in to take it. He made to get down for it, but Ged stopped him. "Leave it. I spent all wizardry at that dry spring, Lebannen. I am no mage now."

Kalessin turned and looked at them sidelong; the ancient laughter was in its eye. Whether Kalessin was male or female, there was no telling; what Kalessin thought, there was no knowing. Slowly the wings lifted and unfurled. They were not gold like Orm Embar's wings but red, dark red, dark as rust or blood or the crimson silk of Lorbanery. The dragon raised its wings, carefully, lest it unseat its puny riders. Carefully it gathered in the spring of its great haunches, and leapt like a cat up into the air, and the wings beat down and bore them above the fog that drifted over Selidor.

Rowing with those crimson wings in the evening air Kalessin wheeled out over the open sea, and turned to the east, and flew.

In the days of high summer on the island of Ully a great dragon was seen flying low, and later in Usidero, and in the north of Ontuego. Though dragons are dreaded in the West Reach, where people know them all too well, yet after this one had passed over and the villagers had come out of their hiding places, those who had seen it said, "The dragons are not all dead, as we thought. Maybe the wizards are not all dead, either. Surely there was a great splendour in that flight; maybe it was the Eldest."

Where Kalessin touched to land none saw. In those far islands there are forests and wild hills to which few men ever come, and where even the descent of a dragon might go unseen.

But in the Ninety Isles there was screaming and disarray. Men rowed westward among the little islands crying, "Hide! Hide! The Dragon of Pendor has broken his word! The Archmage has perished, and the Dragon is come devouring!"

Without landing, without looking down, the great iron-coloured worm flew over the little islands and the little towns and farms, and deigned not even a belch of fire for such small fry. So it passed over Geath, and over Serd, and crossed the straits of the Inmost Sea, and came within sight of Roke.

Never in the memory of man, scarcely in the memory of

legend, had any dragon braved the walls visible and invisible of the well-defended isle. Yet this one did not hesitate, but flew on ponderous wings and heavily over the western shore of Roke, and above the villages and fields, to the green hill that rises over Thwil town. There at last it stooped softly to the earth, and raised its red wings and folded them, and crouched on the summit of Roke Knoll.

The boys came running out of the Great House. Nothing could have stopped them. But for all their youth they were slower than their Masters, and came second to the Knoll. When they came the Patterner was there, come from his Grove, his fair hair bright in the sun. With him was the Changer, who had returned two nights before in the shape of a great sea-osprey, lame-winged and weary; long he had been caught by his own spells in that form, and could not come into his own shape again until he came into the Grove, on that night when the balance was restored and the broken was made whole. The Summoner, gaunt and frail, only one day risen from his bed, had come; and beside him stood the Doorkeeper. And the other Masters of the Isle of the Wise were there.

They saw the riders dismount, one aiding the other. They saw them look about with a look of strange contentment, grimness, and wonder. The dragon crouched like stone while they clambered down from its back and stood beside it. It turned its head a little while the Archmage spoke to it, and briefly answered him. Those who watched saw the sidelong look of the yellow eye, cold and full of laughter. Those who understood heard the dragon say, "I have brought the young king to his kingdom, and the old man to his home."

"A little farther yet, Kalessin," Ged replied. "I have not gone where I must go." He looked down at the roofs and towers of the Great House in the sunlight, and he seemed to smile a little. Then he turned to Arren, who stood tall and slight, in worn clothes, and not wholly steady on his legs from the weariness of the long ride and the bewilderment of all that had passed. In the sight of them all there Ged knelt to him, down on both knees, and bowed his grey head.

Then he stood up and kissed the young man on the cheek, saying, "When you come to your throne in Havnor, my lord and dear companion, rule long, and well."

He looked again at the Masters and the young wizards and the boys and the townsfolk gathered on the slopes and at the foot of the Knoll. His face was quiet, and in his eyes there was something like that laughter in the eyes of Kalessin. Turning from them all he mounted up again by the dragon's foot and shoulder, and took his seat reinless between the great peaks of the wings, on the neck of the dragon. The red wings lifted with a drumming rattle, and Kalessin the Eldest sprang into the air. Fire came from the dragon's jaws, and smoke, and the sound of thunder and the storm-wind was in the beating of its wings. It circled the hill once and flew off, north and eastward, towards that quarter of Earthsea where stands the mountain isle of Gont.

The Doorkeeper, smiling, said, "He has done with doing. He goes home."

And they watched the dragon fly between the sunlight and the sea till it was out of sight.

The Deed of Ged tells that he who had been Archmage came to the crowning of the King of All the Isles in the Tower of the Sword in Havnor at the world's heart. The song tells that when the ceremony of the crowning was over and the festival began, he left the company and went down alone to the port of Havnor. There lay out on the water a boat, worn and beaten by storm and the weather of years; she had no sail up, and was empty. Ged called the boat by name, *Lookfar*, and she came to him. Entering the boat from the pier Ged turned his back on land, and without wind or sail or oar the boat moved; it took him from harbour and from haven, westward among the isles, westward over sea; and no more is known of him.

But in the island of Gont they tell the story otherwise, saying that it was the young King, Lebannen, who came seeking Ged to bring him to the coronation. But he did not find him at Gont Port or at Re Albi. No one could say where he was, only that he had gone afoot up into the forests of the mountain. Often he went so, they said, and did not return for many months, and no man knew the roads of his solitude. Some offered to seek for him, but the King forbade them, saying, "He rules a greater kingdom than do I." And so he left the mountain, and took ship, and returned to Havnor to be crowned.

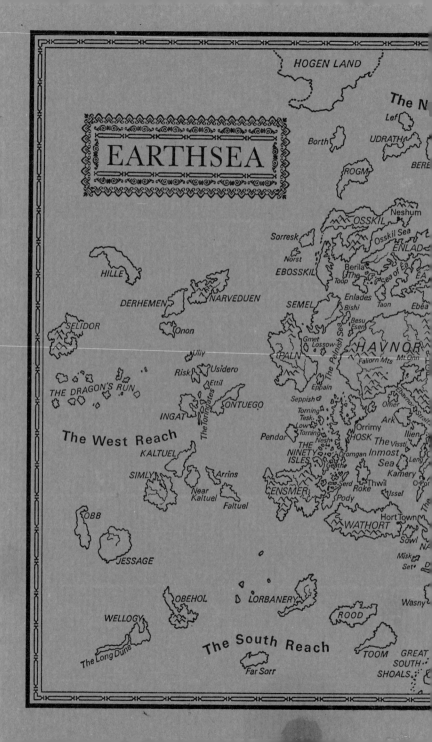